THE
AFTER
OF
US

THE
AFTER
OF
US

S.R. GREY

This is a work of fiction. Names, characters, places, and incidents are products of the author's imagination or are used fictitiously and are not considered to be real. Any resemblance to actual events, locales, organizations, or persons, living or dead, is entirely coincidental.

The After of Us
Copyright © 2016 by S.R. Grey

ISBN-10: 0-9861565-7-4
ISBN-13: 978-0-9861565-7-1

Editing: Hot Tree Editing
Cover Design: Najla Qamber
Cover Photography: CJC Photography
Cover Model: Garrett Finn
Formatting: Tianne Samson with

emtippettsbookdesigns.com

BOOKS BY S.R. GREY

Judge Me Not
I Stand Before You
Never Doubt Me
Just Let Me Love You

The Harbour Falls Mysteries
Harbour Falls
Willow Point
Wickingham Way

Inevitability
Inevitable Detour
Inevitable Circumstances

Laid Bare novella series
Exposed: Laid Bare 1
Unveiled: Laid Bare 2
Spellbound: Laid Bare 3
Sacrifice: Laid Bare 4

Promises series
Tomorrow's Lies

ONE

Will

"COLLEGE graduate, that's me."

It's so hard to believe that I have to utter those words again, out loud, one more time. And then I need more, just to make it really real.

Leaning my head back to stare up at an azure-blue sky, I rise up in the seat of the nice, new BMW convertible I'm driving and scream as loudly as I can, "I'm a goddamn college graduate, motherfuckers."

Take that, all you pricks who didn't believe in me.

I jerk the wheel back just in time to keep from veering off the road, and thus into vast desert nothingness. But yeah, once I'm back on track I think about how no one thought I'd succeed. Not my ex-girlfriend, Cassie, not my mom, and certainly not my stepdad, Greg. I should mention that Greg's not technically my stepdad. Dude never bothered to "officially" adopt me. Not that it matters, not anymore. I'm about to turn twenty-two.

I'm all grown up...and a fucking college grad, as established.

As I hit the gas, the Mojave Desert becomes a hazy blur, my great trek to Las Vegas almost near its end. Yeah, good ole Sin City is where I'm headed. So many Californians take this trip for pleasure. But me, I'm going home.

I estimate I should hit the state line in about another hour—maybe less, at the rate I'm flying—then I'll be back in my home state of Nevada. Of course, I won't be there for long. I'm all set to fly to New York City at the end of the week.

Shit, I have to laugh. I'm a goddamn coming-home success story, if ever there was one. That's right—I, Will Gartner, former fuck-up extraordinaire, have not only graduated from a prestigious college—with honors, no less—but I've also lined up a sweet-ass job in the largest city in the country.

As of next Monday, a week from today, I'll be putting my fancy new graphic design skills—some taught to me at college and others I just have an innate talent for—to work.

And for fat stacks, no less.

When I arrive in New York I'll have a couple of days ahead of me in which to settle in, which is good. Gotta get myself set up in the cool apartment I *think* I want. If I back out, though, it doesn't matter. Mom and Greg have me booked in some fancy Manhattan hotel for however long I need.

Still, what I really want is to do this shit on my own from day one. It's time to cut the ties to my past and quit relying on other people to do shit for me, especially when I can manage things for myself. This is the new me, you see: A Will Gartner who is finally free.

Funny how I don't feel so very free.

I guess I've always seen myself as more of a freelance

kind of artist. My dream was once to publish a comic book line, one I created a long time ago. I used to hope maybe I could turn my early work into a graphic novel, and possibly create a whole series from there. I dreamed of bringing to life in vivid color the characters on my sketch pad, praying one day they'd be seen by others, even if it only ever turned out to be a few.

Oh, well. Guess I'll learn to adjust and be content with the knowledge that my ad work will be viewed by thousands — probably tens of thousands.

Should make me feel good, right?

Yeah, it should. So why is it I feel like nothing but a sellout to corporate greed?

"Quit thinking that stupid idealistic shit," I chastise myself. "Get real."

Refocusing on my itinerary for when I arrive in Vegas, I ponder the one last blowout I plan to have at my parents' house. Not that I've done much planning on it, but the groundwork is set. Mom and Greg are gone, so they aren't a factor. My folks took off for an extended three-month vacation, following my graduation ceremony. That means they won't be back for several weeks. Those two are always traveling, jetting from one place to the next. They were so anxious for this trip to begin that they flew out of LA on Saturday, the day of my graduation. In fact, they even had me drive them to the airport that very night.

I blow out a breath, recalling our final moments at the curb of the passenger drop-off area.

As I helped Mom unload her baggage from the trunk of the graduation present she'd given me — the ice-blue convertible Bimmer I'm driving this very moment — she gave me free rein over her not-so-humble Vegas abode. She has no problem with me staying at her and Greg's oversized McMansion, seeing as I'm about to become what she always dreamed I'd be — a clean-cut business professional.

Nonetheless, my mom, knowing my background and no doubt recalling my reckless younger days, was sure to add, "Have fun, but don't trash the place, Will."

I feigned indignation, placing my hand over my heart and acting hurt. "Would I do such a thing, Mother Dear?"

She gave me a withering look, and Greg chimed in with, "Seriously, Will. No parties."

He returned to his task of loading their bags onto a cart and didn't see me roll my eyes at him. I swear that man will forever view me as fifteen.

Mom, always quick to defend me, dressed Greg down immediately. "Oh, Greg," she said, "a tiny party is fine. My son" — she reached up and ruffled my hair — "can have a few friends over if he likes. I'm sure they'll all behave like perfect ladies and gentlemen."

Ha!

Another eye roll was in order, but I played along, knowing it was to my advantage.

Don't think I can't recognize how fucked up our family dynamic is, with Greg trying to set boundaries and Mom continually shutting him down. That's just her, though. My mom, Abby Gartner Vintner, simply sucks at discipline. I guess that's part of the reason why my brother, Chase, and I had so many problems growing up. Losing our real father and living on the streets for a while didn't help matters, nor did Abby's onetime-pervasive gambling problem, but her overall permissiveness led me and my brother to make a slew of bad choices.

That's all in the past now. Chase is a success story these days.

The one-time felon, who spent four years in prison, runs a thriving business and has a great family. He and his wife, Kay, plus their young children, Jack and Sarah, all came to my graduation this past weekend. They had to fly back directly afterward, however. Chase told me he had work to do on Sunday, something about checking in on a job site that's running behind schedule. He builds homes — like our father once did — in Ohio.

And then there's me. "College graduate," I murmur, savoring the sound of those words one more time.

Still, though. Despite how many times that phrase passes my lips, it just doesn't feel real. But it *is* real. I did it. I survived the fancy school in Malibu that Mom and Greg paid far too much for. And now it's on to the big city to live out my dream.

Or live out someone's dream, a little voice whispers.

"Think about the party," I mutter in response.

Yeah, the party…

I'm thinking one low-key bash at the house won't hurt anyone. No one will probably show up anyway, seeing as I've lost touch with most of my old friends. Probably a good thing, considering how my early high school years were filled with drugs and partying with those exact same people.

Oh, and with my one-time girlfriend, Cassie Sutter.

That chick and I were bad news once we got together. Shit, we were high more often than not. She was my enabler, and I was hers. She also holds claim to the title of "my first love." Walking away from her was one of the hardest things I ever had to do. But if ever there was a toxic love, it was ours.

Think I'm over-exaggerating? I'm not. Hell, I almost killed a man in cold blood for Cassie, if not for Chase intervening.

Chase. Reaching up from the steering wheel, I run my hand through my hair. It's the same light brown color as his. My hair used to be lighter, much lighter. I was once a towheaded blond, back when I was a little kid. My hair also used to be wilder. Not all that long ago, either. Sadly, I had to get a haircut last week, to appear more "professional" for my new job.

What is it that people say? Need to look the part to play the part, right?

Chuckling, I rake my fingers through my hair once more. Thankfully, there's still enough there to grab and pull. Chase does the same thing, all the time. Family trait, I suppose. Wonder if our dad had the same hair-raking quirk?

I can't ask him, seeing as he's dead and gone. Suicide, back when I was eight. My dad drove off a cliff, located in the same exact mountain pass I'll be driving through in roughly thirty minutes.

How fucked up is that? *Thanks, Dad.*

My father, Jack Gartner, is part of the reason why Cassie and I fell in together. She lost her dad when she was young, just like me. And let me tell you, that shared sympathy bonded us hard and tight.

But our woven-together grief, sadly, led to disaster.

On those days when finding solace in each other's arms just wasn't enough, we searched for outside sources to ease the pain. And, oh, did we find shit to do — weed, Oxy, X, cocaine, and other drugs Chase would kill me for if he ever knew I even tried them.

Bad enough he knows what he knows. But there is more, so much more.

Chase also thinks Cass and I never spoke to one another after I broke up with her, back when I was fifteen. For a while, it was true, we didn't talk. I was clean, and Cassie... well, she wasn't. She had done a stint in rehab back when we were in high school, but it didn't stick. Her mom ended up transferring her to a private school on the outskirts of Las Vegas. I guess she was hoping the move would get Cassie in with a different crowd, a straight-laced crew of kids.

It didn't work. Cass was still using, only with a whole new set of people, kids that were far from straight-laced. She still texted me too, all the time, even when I told her I didn't want to see her anymore.

I knew it was time to move on. Like, for real.

But, I had just turned sixteen and was horny as hell. So when Cass started asking me to meet her just to hook up, I'd go.

Every … single … time.

As a result, we ended up having sex all over town — in the backseat of the car my mom had given me for my sixteenth birthday, in alleys where we once scored drugs, and in cheap motels, located in the parts of Vegas tourists never see.

I wasn't doing any drugs that summer. Except for one — Cassie.

I'd given up all the bad things, but I couldn't quite give up on her. Not until her mom found out we were seeing one another did it end. Mrs. Sutter made sure it was over for us when she moved away. Taking Cassie with her, of course.

Off to a different state, they flew. At least I think they settled in a different state. I don't really know for sure. All I *do* know is I haven't seen Cassie since the last day we were together, almost six years ago.

That doesn't mean I still don't think about her from time to time. Not a lot, granted, but sometimes, like now.

I wonder if she ever got her life together, the girl I once loved. I wonder if she got clean. Did she go to college? Maybe she got married? Hell, she could even have a kid by now, for all I know.

But mostly, beyond all those things, I hope my first love found the inner peace she so desperately sought.

TWO

Will

I SPEND the next day just chilling. Mom calls to remind me she has an appointment booked for me with Greg's tailor the following afternoon.

"Oh, joy," I mock.

"Will." Her voice is stern, but there's an underlying excitement. She's amped I'll be wearing suits to work, and it shows when she adds, "I already informed the tailor to put whichever suits you like on my tab. Go and get fitted, and whatever you choose can be sent to you in New York."

"Okay, okay," I acquiesce.

Too bad I don't share my mom's enthusiasm for all this business-man shit.

Nonetheless, like the dutiful son I'm striving to be, I show up at the tailor's on Wednesday afternoon, cheery and ready to get some suits fitted. I even go so far as to don a nice white dress shirt, all crisp and new, so the guy fitting me can get the measurements for my suit jackets exactly right.

I stick with washed jeans on my lower half, though, simply so I still feel like myself.

It all goes smoothly at the tailor's shop, and afterward I stop by the supermarket to pick up some beer for the party tomorrow. The bash is definitely a go for Thursday night. I managed to get word out, albeit on a limited basis. I just don't have the contacts I used to.

At the store, however, I run into an old friend, Nash, who has more than enough contacts to make this party a raging success. Nash is a guy with messy blond hair and surfer-boy good looks. He also possesses killer charm and knows *everyone*.

After the obligatory fist-bump, bro hug, and quick catch-up on what's brought me to town for a few days, he says, "Graduated from Pepperdine, huh? That's cool."

"It is," I agree. "I never thought a kid like me would make it through a school like that."

Nash eyes me curiously then, making a face as he takes in my starched button-down and overall clean-cut appearance. My look is a definite contrast to his long hair, faded board shorts, and ripped tee.

"I'm not surprised," he says quietly. "It seems you've changed a lot."

I let out a nervous chuckle. "Hopefully not too much, man."

It's true; I don't ever want to lose who I am. Though I have changed in good ways, I don't ever plan on ending up being seen as some stuffy, boring dude.

Smoothly switching the subject from me to him, I ask Nash, "So, what've you been up to lately?"

"Oh, hell, not much. Just the same old shit, you know?"

I nod, and he shrugs, the tips of his blond hair brushing at his shoulders. "I was in school for a while," he goes on, "but I ran out of funds. I got a job now, though. Over at that lab on Santa Rosa."

"Oh, yeah," I reply grimly. "I know the place."

I do know the lab, all too well. I was sent to that damn place too many times to count, for piss tests when Mom didn't quite believe I'd quit doing drugs.

Nash rouses me from my reverie when he asks where I'm off to once I leave Las Vegas. I'm happy to talk about something else, so I tell him about my new job.

"Sounds like a great gig," he says, once I'm finished. "When you leaving town?"

"Not till the end of the week. I fly out bright and early on Friday morning."

Nash's eyes — a little blue and a lot bloodshot — take me in once more. "Damn, dude." He points to my shirt that he scowled at earlier and says, "Looks to me like you're ready to leave, like, fucking today."

Laughing, I explain. "My mom made me an appointment with my stepdad's tailor. I just came from there. I was getting fitted for some new suits."

"Wow." Nash snickers. "I can't believe Will Gartner is going to be wearing a suit every day, joining those nine-to-five fuckers. That's pretty unbelievable, man. You know, based on all the crazy shit you used to do."

I can't disagree, so I say, "It is pretty shocking, huh?"

"For sure," he agrees, nodding.

Nash hasn't changed one bit since high school, so I have no hesitation in relaying the details of my party to him. I figure *he* can dig up more party guests, no problem.

I finish up my party-plan spiel with, "So, if you know anyone who might want to stop by the house — "

Nash cuts me off with a wave of his hand. "Say no more, my man." He pats me on the back. "Gartner, dude, I promise you one thing."

"Oh, yeah, what's that?"

"I am going to make it my personal mission that your

last night in this goddamn town is a fucking night to remember."

His words are meant to make me feel good. But suddenly, an impending sense of doom, like my world is about to fall apart, comes over me.

THREE

Will

THE party is in full swing, and I am officially fucked-up.

"Lick..." a sugary voice whispers as a set of double-D tits are thrust in my face. "...right here."

The well-endowed girl — I have no clue of her name — proceeds to straddle me.

"Do it, man."

That's Nash's voice, in the background, urging me on. He brought the girl, along with about a hundred other people. Thank God I had the good sense to cordon off the party zone to the massive pool area in the back of my parents' house.

Salt glistens on the double-Ds in my face, beckoning me to do as the girl has requested — lick.

Ah, hell, who am I to resist?

Leaning forward in a lounger sagging from our weight, I lick and lap at the girl's salty flesh. When I lean back,

Nash hands me another shot of Patrón.

I down the clear liquid in a single gulp.

"Good boy," double-Ds purrs.

She produces a slice of lime from somewhere — maybe from her royal blue bikini bottom? — and holds it out to me, pinched between coral nails.

Before I can accept the lime, she jerks her hand away. "Hey," I protest.

Giggling, she reaches around her back and undoes the tie holding up her bikini top. Next thing I know, she's rubbing the lime wedge all over her wide nipples.

Hungry for her flesh, I lean forward and suck in one sweet-ass, lime-flavored pink areola into my mouth.

"Wanna fuck?" the girl whispers, as I lick and suck and grow hard beneath her wiggling ass.

I do, but I don't.

Releasing her nipple from my mouth, I lean back in the chair. Nash has left. He clearly brought this blonde bimbo for me, as a going-away gift.

Oh, what to do, what to do…?

I scan the area, blinking as I take in all the glowing tiki torches amongst the red-rock grottos and waterfalls. It really is pretty back here, and private, in spots. Despite all the people milling about, there are about a half a dozen secluded grottos interspersed among the large cacti and frilly desert plants. Those grottos are perfect little nooks to sneak into and fuck like animals, if that's what I'm inclined to do — and I sort of am.

Only thing holding me back is that I don't have a condom on me. Up in my room, yes, I have plenty. Unfortunately, though, since I'm comfortable and content underneath this girl, I have no inclination to run inside and tromp all that way up the goddamn stairs.

I could always go bareback.

No, shit, that's the tequila talking. Cassie and I used to

get careless when we were fucked up. But at least I knew she was clean. I'm not about to take that kind of a crazy chance with a stranger. Bad enough I'm already drunk and considering it.

Damn, I'm going to be a wreck tomorrow for my flight.

Sliding the girl down so she's no longer pressing on my hard-on, I politely decline her offer.

"Your loss," she snaps as she re-ties her top and gets up off of me.

"I'm sure it is," I reply, adjusting myself.

Double-Ds-chick takes off, with a huff, and becomes lost in the crowd in no time. I stay in the lounger a while longer, waiting for my dick to calm the fuck down. When I'm no longer sporting noticeable wood, I get up off my ass and make my way to the back door that leads to the kitchen. I need a break from the crowd, and a glass of water would do me a world of good right about now.

No more tequila, I vow, *and no more sucking random tits.*

"But they sure did taste fine," I mutter to myself. *Shit, I really need to get laid.* "Fuck."

In my mom's state-of-the-art kitchen, I turn on the fancy faucet. Lowering my head to the sink, I drink straight from the tap. *Take that for fancy.* I also splash some cold water on my face, hoping to sober up.

I should feel good tonight, but I don't. The party has been fun and all, but I still can't shake that damn feeling of doom that sprung up yesterday at the store.

This is ridiculous.

Probably just my nerves getting the best of me, seeing as I leave to start a brand-new life in less than twelve hours.

I stare out the window above the sink, taking in all the partygoers in the back. There's a lot of drinking going on out there. People are laughing, talking, with little groups convened here and there. At one table, they're passing around a blunt.

God, I want to join them.

I can almost taste the sweet herb and feel the burn in my lungs. And, in that moment, I want to get high, more than anything else.

But that would not be smart.

I can't do it. I just can't. I'm like my brother in that regard — for us, one high is never enough. We seek out the next, and the next, and the next. And I'm *really* bad. Lines of coke, a hit off a pipe containing, well, anything, I have no boundaries once I get going. That's why I completely abstained from drugs at school. I never would have made it to graduation had I started down a path riddled with illegal substances.

Even with legal ones, like alcohol, I have to watch.

That's why I'm in the kitchen right now, away from the booze, away from the drugs, away from girls offering me sex.

"But this is your last night of true freedom, dumbass," I tell myself.

Call it temporary madness, or maybe it's just me flat-out giving in to temptation. I don't know. Blame it on the tequila. Or blame it on my whacked-out nerves. Whatever the case, an urge I can no longer deny compels me to run up to my room and grab a condom from a drawer.

Ten minutes later, I'm in one of those secluded red-rock grottos, far enough from the pool that the splashing sounds are muted. My hands are gripping double Ds' round ass, and my knees are getting chewed up by sand and concrete. But who the fuck cares? Not me, because, damn, my cock feels good, really good. And it looks good too, sliding in and out of a sopping-wet pussy that's doing a damn fine job of making me feel as close to numb as I'm allowed to get this night.

FOUR

Will

I FINALLY discover double-D's name — it's Charlie.

"With an *i-e*," she tells me in a whiny voice as she works on getting dressed. Well, as dressed as one can get donning a string bikini.

"Cool," I reply. "Good to know."

I'm sure I sound distracted, as I'm trying to get my own damn clothes back on.

Charlie — with an *i-e* — stops me, though, just as I'm slipping my tee over my head.

With her hand pressed to my bare chest, she says, "Wait."

"What?" I ask.

She caresses my pecs, *mmm*-ing as she does. "I think we should definitely keep in touch, Will," she says at last.

Not going to happen.

I tug my shirt down over my chest, forcing her hand away. I really am done with this girl, but there's no need to be an outright dick about it.

"Uh, you *do* know I'm leaving for New York City, right?" I say.

This hooking up was a good idea...and a not-so-good idea. Fucking this chick has left me feeling calm and relaxed, sure, but now comes the clingy shit that can make any man question his earlier actions.

"Yeah, I know you're leaving," she replies. "But I'm sure you'll come back to visit your family, right?"

I shrug.

My phone's lying on the ground, having fallen out of my cargo shorts when I shed them in a rush.

Charlie, following my gaze, snatches it up.

"Here..." She starts tapping on the screen. "Let me just add my number to your contacts. No pressure, okay?" — *yeah, right* — "Just think about texting me or calling next time you're in town."

"Sure, okay."

Time to get away.

"You had fun tonight, didn't you?" She raises a brow and gestures to where she was on her hands and knees, taking it like a champ.

I had a fine time, yes, but I downplay it now, lest she start thinking it meant more than it did.

"It was nice, Charlie." I place my hand on the small of her sweaty back and lead her back to the party area. "I better walk around and mingle," I say. "I am leaving, after all. And this is *my* party."

I think she finally gets the hint that I'm trying to let her down easily.

"Oh, okay. That's cool." She peers into the thinning crowd. "Hey, I think I see one of my friends over there, anyway." She starts to walk away, but then falters and looks back at me. Shooting me a small smile, she says, "Bye, Will."

"Yeah, see 'ya."

God, I am such a dick sometimes, even when I'm trying not to be one.

It's late—later than I realized—and people are starting to leave en masse. Nash is one of the last to go, but before he takes off he comes over and wishes me good luck with my new job.

"You have fun with Charlie?" he asks with a conspiratorial wink.

"Yeah," I reply, chuckling. "You could say it was fun."

"Good." He pats me on the back. "Hey, we'll keep in touch, yeah?"

"Sure."

Nash gives me one of his business cards from the lab. "Text me when you're back in town." He waves his hand at a cluster of red plastic cups on one of the tables, unintentionally reminding me that I have a lot of cleaning up to do. "We'll do this again sometime."

"Yeah, sounds good," I tell him.

"Cool. See you around."

And then he's gone.

It's two o'clock in the morning, but since I'm leaving in a few hours, I am far too amped to sleep.

I jog upstairs and take a quick shower to wash away the tequila-laced memories of Miss Double-Ds. Then, I head back outside to start cleaning up the pool area.

FIVE

Will

By three a.m., things are in good order. Good enough, that is. The cleaning lady is due in tomorrow—or, technically, later today—so she can deal with the rest.

Before heading up to bed, I walk around to the front of the house so I can close and lock the heavy wrought iron gates at the end of the driveway. Everything is usually quiet when it's late like this, but tonight there's a yellow cab idling across from the house.

That's odd.

Things grow even stranger when the cabbie rolls down his window and spits out onto the street. This is a nice neighborhood, and shit like that just doesn't happen.

The gates are in the process of closing, but I hit the control panel and stop them mid-swing. "Hey, you lost?" I call over to the grubby driver.

He ignores me completely as he lights up a smoke.

"Dickhead," I mutter under my breath.

Just as I'm turning away, about to hit the command button to close the gates the rest of the way, the back door of the taxi pops open. Out of the corner of my eye, I spot a super-skinny girl with stringy dishwater-blonde hair spilling out onto the road. Like, literally, the chick almost eats concrete.

I walk out to the sidewalk to see what the hell is up.

As the girl rights herself and adjusts the light blue tank top and jean shorts she's wearing, I sense something familiar about her. Unfortunately, there are far too many shadows being cast by the dim glow of the fancy gas street lamps for me to discern if I know this girl...or not.

I'm about to close the gate, for real this time, but just then the scraggly girl starts walking over to where I'm standing. I am afforded a much clearer view, and am soon muttering, "What the...?"

First, it's clear the girl is a druggie. No one clean and sober scratches at their bare arms like this chick's doing, nor do they tug repeatedly and methodically at the hem of their shirt. Oh, and they definitely don't move their mouths in weird ways.

This girl does all of those things. So, yeah, I conclude she's a user.

As she draws nearer and nearer, it hits me — shit, I *know* this girl. Hell, I used to *love* this girl.

"Cassie?" I mutter, amazed and appalled all at the same time.

My ex-girlfriend must've moved back to Las Vegas at some point, but, clearly, things aren't going so well.

Maybe I'm dreaming all this?

I pinch myself. *No, not dreaming.*

As the strung-out girl reaches me, any lingering doubt is erased. This is definitely my one-time girlfriend, my first love, Cassie Sutter.

Fuck, though, man. She sure is a shadow of her former self. If there was ever a reason for me to be grateful I swore off drugs, this is it.

"Will," Cassie says softly when she sees recognition on my face.

Her voice still hints at vulnerability, but there's a hard, gravelly edge that used to not be there.

"Cassie," I croak out as emotions I didn't count on well up. I loved this girl once and, truth is, it hurts to see her like this.

"Hey." She smiles wide, and shit....

The smile I was about to send back falters.

Cassie quickly looks away.

Wow, just wow. And not a good kind of wow. The girl I once loved used to have this gorgeous, all-American smile. Not anymore. Her teeth are now yellowed and stained, and one is flat-out missing.

"God, Cass," I blurt out without thinking. "What the hell happened to you?"

Her head jerks back to me sharply. "Nice to see you, too," she snaps, her tone dripping with sarcasm.

I barely hear her. All I can think is that Cassie needs help. Like, immediately. Her addiction is spinning out of control.

"You want me to take you to a hospital or something?" I offer. "You can check in for a psych evaluation. You might even be able to slip into a rehab center as early as tom—"

Cassie recoils like I smacked her. "Rehab? Psych evaluation? I don't need those things, Will."

Scoffing, I say, "Uh, actually, I think you do, Cassie."

And just like that, she's infuriated. "Jesus, you're still such an arrogant prick. You always were. Have you forgotten *your* past? Like *you* never got fucked up?" She lets out a nasty cackle. "I, for one, know you did just as many drugs as me."

"It was never like this," I maintain as I strive to remain calm. "I wasn't a junkie."

"I'm not a junkie," she hisses. "And, you know what? Fuck you, Will. Just fuck you." She throws her hands in the air. "This was a mistake. I never should've come here."

"Why *are* you here, anyway?" I shoot back. "Showing up at my house at three in the morning? What the hell could *you* possibly want from *me* after all these years?"

This is how it got at the end of our relationship. We were always bickering, always snapping at each other.

But, really, *why* is she here?

I always thought if I ever ran into Cassie someday she'd be this beautiful older version of the cute, quirky teen I used to know—the girl with ethereal features, tiny and small, all wispy blonde hair and translucent skin. I guess I always imagined her clean and leading a normal life.

And this is *so* not that version. This Cassie makes me sad. And I really do want to help, if she'll let me.

"Look, I'm sorry, okay?" I swallow twice to keep my voice even. This is upsetting on so many levels, but I don't want to show her how distraught I really feel. It will only upset her further.

"Seriously, Cass," I continue after a beat. "If you're coming to me, I can only guess it's because you want my help in some way."

Our eyes meet, and for, like, a minute, I see the old Cassie. Despite the fact her pale blues are unfocused and distant.

"Let me help," I whisper, hoping to break through her defenses. "Please."

There is a part of me that will always care for Cassie. I loved her first, and I loved her hard.

She sniffs and rubs her nose, and then she looks away.

"I do need your help with something," she says at last, the moment lost. "But what I want from you has nothing to do with psych evals and fucking rehab."

She's not going to let me help her, not with the drug issue, anyway.

Sighing, I fold my arms across my chest. "What is it you want, then?" It finally dawns on me that someone must have told her I was in town. "How'd you know I'd be here at the house? I was in California until just the other day."

"I know." She smiles again, but carefully, so as not to expose her teeth this time. "But word got out that you were back," she tells me.

"What do you mean, 'word got out'? You stay in touch with our old friends?"

I'm suspicious, as not a soul mentioned Cassie earlier tonight. Was this some kind of setup?

Cassie must remember my "tells"—the little quirks that always gave away what I was thinking—as she's quick to say, "This wasn't planned, Will. No one was "in" on me showing up, okay? That's why I waited for the party to clear out."

"You knew about the party?"

Chuckling, she lifts her hand to show me a scratched-up, beaten-to-hell-and-back smartphone. "I like to stay up-to-date with social media, though I really don't know why. It's not like I ever talk to anyone we used to know—not anymore. I guess old habits die hard, you know?" She blows out a breath. "Anyway, I still follow a few people. Someone mentioned something about your party on Twitter." She purses her lips. "Or maybe it was on Facebook."

I raise a brow. "Was it Nash?"

Cassie nods. "Yeah, I think it was his page I was looking at."

Of course, after I asked, Nash would've posted news of my party all over social media. That's why so many people showed up on such short notice. And that's how Cassie knew I'd be here.

But she obviously had no interest in the party, so again I ask, "Why are you here, Cass?"

She glances over at the cab. The driver still has his window down and, although there's no way he can hear us, he gives Cassie a shrug and an accompanying questioning look.

"You know him?" I ask, jerking my chin to the cab.

"He's a friend."

Cassie digs a little white pill from the front pocket of her shorts. When she pops it into her mouth, I am stunned. She looks high enough already.

"Hey. What the hell are you doing?" I ask.

She tilts back her head and swallows. "I need it for what I'm about to do."

"Okay, Cass." I am beyond wary now. "What the fuck is up?"

She gestures to the driver, prompting him to twist around and speak to someone in the back seat.

What the…?

Just as I'm about to lose my shit over all this elusive bull, the back door of the cab opens unsteadily.

And then a little girl clambers out.

What the hell is a kid doing up at this time of the night?

Cassie's whole demeanor softens. "Come on over, baby. Come meet the guy I told you about, the nice man named Will."

"Whoa." I take a step back, completely thrown. "You have a kid?"

What must life be like for this poor child? I dealt with a mom who was battling addiction—gambling, though, not drugs. Nonetheless, it was hell.

"Yeah…" Cassie nods, her eyes glued to the small girl lingering uncertainly by the cab. "I have a kid."

Addressing the little girl, Cassie yells across the street, "Get over here, Lily."

Despite the fact not one car has gone by, the little girl looks both ways before crossing. She is a cute little thing, tiny as all get out, and with a full head of long, platinum-blonde hair. She's wearing a lavender tee that has "Princess" spelled out in sequins, and jean shorts that match her mom's. There's also a pink backpack on her back. I can't pin the ages of kids too precisely, but this one looks to be about five or six.

Her blonde hair blows in the light breeze as she runs over to us, and when she reaches Cassie, she takes her hand and peers up at me curiously. "Hi," the little girl says.

"Uh," is about all I can get out, seeing as I'm struck speechless by this kid's eyes.

Her eyes are an all-too-familiar green, vivid and bright, like the shade of young grass in the spring. Eyes like—

"Is this my daddy, Mommy?"

"Yes, Lily. This is your dad."

SIX

Cassie

NEVER wanted to do this to Will. Not in this way.

Oh, the look on his face.

He doesn't deserve to find out he's a father in this manner. Will was always a good guy. And I loved him once, I really did. I tell Lily all the time she was created from love, from something that was once beautiful. Too bad all she's been exposed to living with me lately is the ugly side of life.

That's why I *have* to do this. I've thought about it before, but this is my chance. The only opportunity I may ever have to do what's best for my little girl.

"You have to take her, Will." It's not a request, it's a heartfelt plea. "She'll have a better life with you."

"*What?*"

Poor guy looks stunned. My own heart is breaking, but I'm too numb to let it bother me very much. "I'm sorry," I say.

"Sorry? Cass, are you crazy?" Will looks from me to Lily, then back to me. "Tell me this is a joke. Something Nash put you up to. It's a going-away prank, right?"

Will knows it's not a joke, but just to be sure he's clear, I state, "It's not a prank. Lily is yours, Will. Just look at her."

He does, and I know he sees himself in her eyes. I see the same thing every day, or at least during the days I'm around Lily. Our daughter has Will's eyes, for sure, the same shade of green as his mother's. And there's more. Back when we were dating, Will once showed me pictures that were taken when he was little. The super-blonde hair Lily has is the same exact color Will once sported.

Yeah, there's no denying that my daughter—*our* daughter—is the spitting image of a five-year-old Will.

Angry that he can no longer deny it, Will spits out, "You never thought to tell me before today?"

"I wanted to, but my mom stopped me. You remember how it was. She made us cut all ties."

"How old is Lily?" he asks, his voice shaky and his eyes glued to his child. "Five?"

I know he's calculating, making sure she's his. "Yes, she's five."

"When's her birthday?"

"March twentieth."

He swallows hard. "So, it happened when we used to meet, after we broke up?"

There's resignation in his voice, acceptance of what I'm telling him. He knows we weren't careful at the end.

"Yeah," I confirm. "It happened then."

Softly, he sighs. "Okay, but... I can't take her, Cassie. I *won't* take her. You're her mom, she should stay with you."

"No, Will. No." I am adamant. I'm not budging, not on this. My daughter deserves better than what I give her.

"Cassie," he begins.

There's reluctance in his tone, and I wave my hands around, frustrated. "You have to take her, Will. The way I live…" I trail off, sigh, begin again. "Okay, I admit that I probably do too many drugs. And I know it's not good for a little girl to be around that kind of shit."

It's so hard to say it out loud, but the truth is I know my drug use is out of control, despite denying it to Will mere minutes ago.

"Besides," I continue, pointing to his mom's ostentatious house, half-hidden behind the partially closed gate. "Your family has lots of money. Plus, Nash mentioned in one of his posts that you landed a big-time job. I have nothing to offer Lily, Will. You, though… You have everything. She should be with you."

"I stay with Daddy now?" Lily asks in a barely audible voice.

Her little kid tone is so matter-of-fact that I cringe with disappointment, in myself. I'm such a bad mother. My daughter is so used to being shuffled around that it's barely registering with her that we'll be apart, yet again.

Truth is I hardly know my daughter. I've spent so little time with her. My mom had Lily for a long time, throughout all my failed stints in rehab, and all the times I just felt overwhelmed and bolted. But my mother finally got fed up with me. She was planning to fight me for custody, and that's why I took off for good…with Lily. It's also how I landed back in Vegas. But, like I said, I'm not around Lily as much as I should be. I have to work, you know. And after my shift is done at the club, I need to let off some steam. Lily can't come with me to the parties I like to go to.

"Lily is used to staying with other people," I tell Will. "She'll be a good girl for you." I stare down at my daughter. "Won't you, Lil?"

She nods. "I be good."

Before Will can respond and put a stop to me leaving Lily with him, I say, "Lily loves to color and draw." I tap the pink backpack strapped to her back. "Her coloring books and crayons are in here. Sit her down with those things and she'll be content for hours."

Lily peers up at me, hanging on my every word. She's a smart kid, and somewhere inside she probably senses I'm leaving her for good. Will is all she has now.

I have to look away. I need another hit of something so I don't feel so damn guilty.

While I stare over at the cab, where I know my cabbie friend, Niko, has more drugs, I hear Lily say to Will, "I'll behave, I promise. I stay with Mommy's friends *a lot*, and I'm always a good girl."

There's desperation in Lily's voice. She's caught on that this is it. It's her dad or probably foster care. Child services have been sniffing around lately, and it hasn't gone unnoticed by Lily.

Will snorts, disgusted with me. He shoots me a look like he'd like to strangle me. *Good, maybe now it'll register with him how fucked up I am and he'll take his kid.*

"You leave Lily with strangers?" he asks tightly.

"Not strangers," I say, miffed. "I have lots of friends, Will."

"Druggies, I'm sure. Like you."

Will is seething now. Fine, I need him mad. I need him to keep Lily. Maybe someday I'll get clean and want her back, but I can't see that happening anytime soon. Truth is I'm just not mom material, nor do I really care to be.

Okay, all I want now is to get the hell out of here. I'm antsy, and I need another hit of something, anything. That stupid pill I took is doing nothing.

Tapping my foot anxiously, I ask, "So, you'll keep her, yeah?"

Will's expression is grim, resigned. "I'm not staying in Vegas," he says. "My job's on the East Coast."

"I know," I say. And I do. The farther Lily is from me, the better off she'll be.

I've backed Will into a corner, so, again, I press, "It's decided, then, right? Lily can stay with you?"

"For now, yeah, okay."

Ha, this is more permanent than he thinks.

I give Niko a thumbs-up, and he hops out of the cab with Lily's small pink suitcase in tow. It matches her backpack, and that makes me smile. But when Niko walks over and hands the damn thing to me, I feel nothing but sadness.

Before my own conscience can stop me, I turn the suitcase over to Will. Meanwhile, Niko jogs back over to the cab, having never acknowledged anyone but me.

"Nice guy," Will snaps, his tone icy and dripping with sarcasm as he sets the suitcase down on the sidewalk.

"He's a good dude," I counter.

I don't add that my opinion is colored by the fact Niko shares his drugs with me. Doesn't matter what I say, or don't say, Will sees the truth in my eyes. "I'm sure he's just a peach," he mutters dryly.

I ignore Will and crouch down to Lily's height. "Give Mommy a kiss good-bye."

My little girl touches her soft lips to mine. "Love you, Mommy."

"I'll miss you so much, baby."

I fight back tears. Why is this hard? This shouldn't be hard, dammit.

Lily pulls away and eyes me curiously. She's always been a perceptive child, and now is no exception. "You come back for me soon?" she asks warily.

There's no point in lying. "I don't think so, Lily. You're going to be staying with Will now."

"Like I used to stay with Nana?"

I nod. "Yes, exactly like that. Will's your daddy, like I told you on the way over. Remember how I also mentioned how sad it's been that you two have never had a chance to get to know each other?"

"Mommy, I'd rather stay with you."

I speak right over my daughter's distressed words. "You living with Will, Lily," —I try to smile, but can't— "this is your chance and his to, like, bond or whatever."

I can't look at Will, but I feel his fury—fury directed at me—for discarding my daughter in this way. Well, she's his daughter too, and it's his turn to take care of her.

Lily nods, acquiescing at last, but I see her swallowing hard. "Okay, Mommy," she whispers.

"Doesn't mean I don't love you, baby girl," I assure her.

"I know, Mommy."

Her affect is flat, the emotion drained from her voice. Lily is shutting down on me. And she should. I suck at this mom thing.

I stand up and tell Will, "Hey, look, I gotta go."

And then, before he can reply, I'm running across the street, as fast as I can, away from a boy I used to love, away from the daughter I'm abandoning.

Will is yelling now, saying things like, he needs my number. And other shit too: what if there's an emergency or he needs to contact me. *No way.*

Niko welcomes me back in the cab, and I blurt out in a rush, "Go, go, go."

He hits the gas and hands me a meth pipe. I reach for a lighter. The whole time I look forward. Not once do I look back.

SEVEN

Will

WATCH as the cab takes off with Cassie. *Fuck.* I am so fucked. How can I be a dad? This can't be happening. This must be what that bad feeling, the one I had all yesterday and today, was trying to tell me. My world really *is* falling apart.

Shit.

Not only am I stuck with a little girl whom I have no idea how to take care of, but I also have no way to contact Cassie. What if there's an emergency? Or, what if I have a question about Lily's care? What if it all gets to be too much and I need to send her back?

To a druggie mom? My conscience tsks at me.

"Yeah, maybe not," I mutter.

Still, I am so fucked.

"Where we go now?" Lily asks, breaking me from my reverie.

She's peering up at me with those familiar green eyes,

and my heart melts a little. She really is a little doll.

Crouching down to her level, I ask her, "Do you know where you and your mommy live?"

I have no plans to take Lily back, but it'd be nice to know where I can find Cassie, just in case.

Lily points in the direction the cab took off. "That way?"

It's a question, not an answer. The little thing has no clue. And how could she? She's only five.

I pat her tiny shoulder. *Jeez, she's small.* "It's okay. We'll figure it out later."

Sighing, I pick up Lily's small suitcase and gesture to the house behind the half-closed gates. "You ready to go inside?"

She peers past me at the huge house, eyes wide. "You live in that big house?"

"Yes." I then correct myself, since kids take things so literally. "Well, I mean my parents live in that house. I'm only staying here one more night. I'm supposed to leave tomorrow for New York City to start a new job." Sighing, I add, "I guess you'll be coming with me now."

Lily nods, all easy-going, and I almost have to laugh at her adult-like contemplative expression. "Okay," she agrees. "I can go with you."

Like not going with me was ever an option.

Taking her small hand in mine, I say, "Come on. Let's go inside."

In the spacious foyer, I let go of Lily's hand so I can check the time. *Shit.* It's nearly four in the morning. I have to be at the airport by nine at the latest if I'm to make the ten o'clock flight I'm scheduled to be on. There are also some new logistics I need to work out. Like, who's going to watch Lily while I'm at work? The ad agency already warned me to expect to work *way* past five every day of the work week.

"Damn you, Cassie," I mutter, indecipherably, on purpose.

"I can't hear you," Lily says.

"It was nothing," I reply.

I set her suitcase on the marble floor and walk around the room, turning on lights, including the large crystal chandelier directly above Lily. She peers up, awe evident in her expression. She then scans the opulent foyer. Her green eyes, which match mine, just about bulge out of her head.

The house is impressive, surely even to a kid, especially one who's most likely been living in squalor. Apart from the glittering chandelier, there's a huge spiral staircase to Lily's right, pricey paintings on all the walls, and richly toned marble everywhere.

"Your house is so pretty, Daddy," Lily says with awe.

I wince at the "daddy" part. I don't even know this kid yet. And though her eyes match mine—and I can't deny she resembles me in other ways, like the hair—I have every intention of getting a DNA test.

Despite all my internal bluster, I just *know* she's mine. "Still," I whisper.

Lily, losing interest in the impressive foyer, asks, "Hey, do you like to draw?"

Smiling, I reply, "Funny you should ask, but I actually do like to draw."

Yet another similarity between me and this kid. *Shit.*

Lily shrugs off her backpack. "You do coloring, too?"

"Eh, that, not so much."

She places her backpack on the floor, unzips it, and pulls out a coloring book. "You want to color with me?" Peering down at the Disney-themed book, she adds, "You can draw stuff in here too, if you want. I draw in the empty spaces all the time. Mommy calls it dood-da-ling."

"Aren't you tired, Lily?" I ask.

Truth is I'm a little stunned this little girl seems not one bit bothered by the late hour.

Lily shakes her head. "No."

"Does your mommy let you stay up late like this a lot?"

She nods, and I roll my eyes. "Hey," I begin, "I think maybe we better hold off on coloring till tomorrow, okay?"

"'Kay," Lily reluctantly agrees, clearly disappointed, as she slides the coloring book back into her backpack.

Sighing, I say, "We need to get some sleep, Lily. It's really, really late."

"Uh-huh."

She still sounds so down, so I try turning this clusterfuck into something fun. "Oh, and hey, guess what?"

"What?"

"You are about to have the honor of picking out whichever bedroom you want to stay in. Any at all, Lily, and we have lots and lots to choose from."

Lily says, "Okay," but it's uttered with no enthusiasm whatsoever.

I watch as she stares down blankly at the marble floor. This has to be really tough on her, too. She may be accustomed to being shuffled from place to place, but Cassie made it clear those times were always only for a few nights. This situation is going to last for more than a few nights, and Lily knows it. Guess it's really sinking in now.

Smiling as kindly as I can, I grab up her backpack and take her little hand in mine. I then lead her up the stairs so she can choose a room to sleep in for the night.

Lily ends up picking out a bedroom decorated in loads of purple tones, which she informs me is her favorite color. "I kind of guessed that from your shirt," I say.

She glances down at her lavender top. "Oh."

"Come on, Lily."

I help her settle into bed, and then turn off the light.

But before I'm out the door, I hear her whimpering.

Flicking the switch back on, I ask, "Is something wrong?"

"Yes," she whispers. "I'm scared of the dark."

"Oh, okay." I walk back into the room and turn on a small lamp that's near the bed. "That better?"

"Uh-huh."

Again, I try to leave, and again I am stopped by a small pleading voice. "I'm scared to be alone, too."

I sit down on the edge of the bed. "I thought you told me you're used to staying with other people?"

"I am, but"—she spreads her arms out as far as she can—"your house is so *huge*. What if I can't find you? Where do you sleep, anyway?"

Pointing to the doorway, I say, "I'll be just down the hall."

Lily sits up and starts rubbing her eyes fiercely. And then she starts to cry. "Mommy's not coming back for me *ever*, is she?"

I tell her the truth. "I don't know, Lily. She may not. Or, if she *does* come back, it probably won't be for a very long while."

That makes Lily cry harder, and I silently curse Cassie. I rub the kid's shoulder, but that doesn't help. It's only when I hold her in my arms that she quiets.

It's awkward at first. The only kids I'm ever really around are Chase and Kay's son and daughter. And though I give Jack and Sarah plenty of hugs, I never really hold them—not like this.

After a few minutes of comforting Lily, it starts to feel natural. Maybe deep inside, on some primal level, I know she's mine. What I do know is she smells really good, all fresh and new and clean.

When I lean down to kiss the top of her head, I realize she's fallen asleep. Gently, I ease her down to the pillows.

I don't close the door all the way. I leave it open a crack, in case Lily needs me before morning.

Morning… What am I going to do about tomorrow?

In my room, I fire up my laptop.

Flying to New York City in a few hours is just not going to happen. I can delay looking at the apartment I'm interested in for a couple of days. I start the new job on Monday, though, and I can't miss my first day.

And what am I going to do about Lily?

I clearly need time to set things up. Didn't I hear somewhere that securing good daycare in New York City is a bitch?

If only someone could watch Lily for a while, like maybe for the summer.

"Chase," I say out loud, as an idea is born.

Yeah, maybe Chase and Kay can take care of Lily. It'd only be for a short while. They have kids her age. Jack is five, like Lily, and Sarah is what? Four, I think. *Perfect.* It's June, and there should be lots of kid things to do throughout an Ohio summer. Chase would know more about that. And Kay's a stay-at-home mom these days. Plus, there's all that extra room in their big farmhouse in Harmony Creek. Surely, my brother and his wife will be cool with this.

Quickly, I book flights for Lily and me to fly into the newly opened regional airport in Harmony Creek on Saturday. I then cancel my flight to NYC, the one that's to leave in a few hours, and book a flight instead for Sunday night out of Ohio.

Good, all set.

Still, I don't forget about the first order of business for tomorrow. Before I go to bed, I type out a text to Nash: *Hey, any way you can expedite a DNA test?*

EIGHT

Will

DNA *test? Dude. WTF is up?*

That's the text I wake up to. It's too complicated to reply with all the details, so I just call Nash.

Once I explain the situation, he tells me, "Yeah, sure. Go ahead and bring the kid in. It's a simple mouth swab for both of you. And I'll do what I can to get the results back pronto."

"Thanks for doing me this solid, man."

"Not a problem."

"Not a problem" may be the case when it comes to my business with Nash, but I soon discover it sure is a problem, a big problem, trying to get Lily up and out of bed.

"I don't wanna," she cries after I ask her to get up for, like, the tenth time. Burrowing under the covers, I hear her, tone muffled, state, "I told you I'm sleepy."

I've tried cajoling and pleading. Now it's time to get

serious.

"Come on, Lily," I say in a stern tone that reminds me of my dad—my real dad, not Greg. "We have to leave soon."

She peeks out from under the covers. "Where we have to go?" she asks warily.

"We have an appointment this afternoon. So, you need to get up so you can shower and dress."

"I *am* dressed," she yells belligerently.

She's got me there. Oops, I forgot to make her change into pajamas. She still has on the purple "Princess" tee and jean shorts she was wearing last night.

I try another tactic. "Well, I bet you're hungry. And if you get out of that bed right now, I'll make us something yummy to eat. Okay?"

No response.

"Oh," I add, "you should probably still take a shower, maybe put on some clean clothes. You want to be fresh and ready for the day, right?"

When she fails to respond a second time, I pull the covers off her in one fell swoop. Lily absolutely does not like that. She kicks and screams for all she's worth.

Damn, she seemed like such an easy-going kid last night. What the hell happened?

Sprinkled between her crying jags, my little monster of a daughter informs me that she doesn't take showers. "I'm a little kid, dummy dumbhead stupid. I take baths!"

"Don't call your father names like that." *Is this me, Will Gartner, really uttering those words?*

"Dummy, dumbhead, stupid, dummy."

I make her sit up, dodging her slaps. "Quit trying to hit me, Lily."

"I hate you!" she screams.

This is definitely Cassie's daughter. It's time to find out if she really is mine, as well.

I finally get her out of bed, but she refuses to change her clothes. I throw up my hands. "Whatever, I give up."

With all the confusion, we end up running late. There's no time for me to make breakfast, so I take us through a fast food drive-thru on the way to the lab.

Lily spills juice in my new BMW and gets hash brown crumbs everywhere, but I bite my tongue. She's behaving for the moment, so why rock the boat?

Before we head into the lab, and while I'm unbuckling her seat belt, she informs me, "That was fun. I never sit in a car like a grown-up before."

"Oh, shit." I need to get a car seat, like, as soon as possible.

"You swore." Lily giggles.

I'm batting a thousand at this dad thing. Not.

Lily is great in the lab; she thinks getting her cheek swabbed is a blast. Nash gives her a lollipop afterward, and she's content with that while I get my own cheek swabbed.

Nash informs me before I leave that he'll rush the results. "I could have them as early as this evening," he tells me. "If so, I'll give you a call. But, dude…" He lowers his voice to a whisper, so Lily doesn't hear. "…that kid looks too much like you not to be yours. Check out her eyes."

Sighing, I say, "I know. I did."

Lily looks up at me then, lips stained purple from the grape lollipop. I can't help but smile. "What, Daddy?" she asks.

Again with the daddy thing, though it *is* growing on me.

I shake my head. "It's nothing, sweetheart." I take her small hand in mine. "You ready to go?"

She nods and blinks up at me with those all-too-familiar greens.

Nash calls that night, and it's no surprise at all when he says, "Lily's definitely yours, man."

So, I, without a doubt, have a kid. The lab results confirm what I already knew in my heart. Still, this makes it undisputable.

I call Chase.

"Hey," I say — too enthusiastically, probably — as soon as he answers. "How was your flight back to Ohio last weekend?"

I'm not one to call and ask about shit like this, so Chase is immediately suspicious. He knows I'm a sneak.

"Uh, it was good," he says slowly. "Jack and Sarah were surprisingly well-behaved, even though we had a long delay in Dallas."

"Ah, yeah," I drone on as I try to put off the inevitable. "That's where your connecting flight went through, right?"

Chase sighs. "Will, what's going on?"

He knows me all too well.

"Uh, I got something I need to ask you."

"Shoot."

"Would it be okay with you if I flew out to Harmony Creek tomorrow? You know, to visit with you guys?"

"Uh—"

I speak right over my brother, lest he quash my plan before he hears all of it. "I was thinking maybe we could spend my last day and a half of freedom hanging out and shit. You know, like old times?"

Chase hesitates, surely suspicious, but eventually says, "Yeah, sure, Will. Though I thought you were planning to fly into New York City early to look at apartments? Don't you start the new job this Monday?"

I blow out a breath. This may be harder to pull off than I imagined.

"Yeah, yeah, I do, that's true." I nod, even though Chase can't see me. "But, I figure Mom has me booked at a hotel for however long I want. So, there's no real rush to find a place to live. Besides…" My voice goes up a notch as I feign excitement. "…I'd much rather spend some quality time with my brother and his awesome family."

Like that doesn't sound shady.

Surprisingly, Chase buys it.

He must be tired, probably worn out from his kids. Now that I see how exhausting one can be, I can only imagine what it'd be like dealing with two little people who seem to need something every sec.

"Okay. Sounds great, Will," Chase says. "It'll be nice to see you again before you get too bogged down with work."

He sounds so sincere that I start to feel like a real dick.

"Yeah, exactly what I was thinking." Hurriedly, I add, "So, anyway, my flight is due to arrive sometime around dinner."

"What?" Chase sounds shocked. "You mean you already booked a flight?"

"Uh, yeah. Is that okay? I guess I was counting on you being cool with me visiting."

"Of course it's fine, Will. I'm just a little surprised, that's all." Chase sighs. "So, do you want me to pick you up at the airport?"

Hell, I definitely don't want Chase coming to the airport. Best to spring Lily on him at his house, with Kay around, so she can keep him calm.

"No. I'll just rent a car," I reply as nonchalantly as I can muster

"Okay, then. Guess we'll see you tomorrow, Will."

Yeah, they sure will. I just hope my brother doesn't kill me when he finds out I have a daughter…and that I plan to leave her with him and his family for the entire summer.

NINE

Will

Who knew traveling with a kid could be so, uh, challenging. It seems like Lily needs something every ten minutes.

"Daddy, I'm hungry."

I give her a couple of apple slices I wisely packed in my carry-on for a snack.

"I can't find my coloring book."

I dig one out from the bottom of her backpack.

"Not this one."

Ugh. "Lily, your other coloring books are in your suitcase, along with the rest of the luggage we checked."

"Where's my suitcase?"

I count to ten. "I just told you where it is. In the cargo hold, with everyone else's checked bags."

"What's 'checked' mean?"

"Lily" — I hand her some crayons — "just color, okay?"

"My favorite blue crayon isn't with these ones." She

scrunches up her face, holding the offending Crayolas aloft. "I can't color without my best crayon, Daddy."

More digging in the backpack, till I finally find the damn blue crayon. "Here," I say.

"Nooo! Not this one!"

I keep digging, holding yet another blue crayon out to her. "Is this sky-blue the one you want?

"Yes." She shoots me an adorable grin. "Thanks, Daddy."

"You're welcome, Lil."

I sneak in an eight-minute nap. And then: "I have to pee."

I walk Lily to the lavatory in the back of the plane, and ask when we reach our destination, "Are you okay with going in there by yourself?"

Lily nods. "You wait out here, though, okay?"

"You got it."

Despite her needing a lot from time to time, like today, Lily is surprisingly self-sufficient. She used the bathrooms in the house just fine, even dragged a stool from the corner of the powder room attached to the guest bedroom she was staying in so she could reach the sink to wash her hands after she was done.

And, I'm proud to say that last night I scored my first dad victory when I convinced Lily to take a bath. She refused to let me stay in the room, though, so I was mindful to make sure the water in the tub remained low. I waited outside the door in case she needed me, but she was a trooper. Lily came out with pajamas on and everything, although her top was inside out and her hair was all tangled. I let her keep her shirt on wrong, but spent twenty minutes combing gently through her blonde locks.

I smile now at the memory. Despite some bratty moments, she's a sweet kid.

Something pulls at my heart, and I can't deny that it's

going to suck to leave her. But it's best she stay with Chase and Kay this summer, since I won't be around enough. Who knows, though? Maybe I could fly in on weekends to visit with her.

When we return to our seats, Lily contents herself with coloring in her book. I'm amazed at how well she stays within the lines. I notice, on some pages, someone has added extra detail in the spaces where there's nothing to color. Just a few simple flowers and basic trees here and there, but damn if the lines and proportions aren't spot-on.

I point to a close-to-perfect daisy. "Who drew that?" I ask Lily.

"I draw it," she says, without bothering to look up from where she's intensely coloring a bluebird.

"Wow."

Lily must be like me and Chase. We both have crazy-good talent when it comes to creating art. It looks like she's definitely inherited that particular Gartner gene, as it's showing up in her drawing at an early age.

Speaking of all things Gartner, I was surprised this morning to discover Cassie gave Lily *my* last name. I found her birth certificate in a pocket on her suitcase when I was searching for her ID.

Shit, to think for five years this little girl has been walking around with my name, and I didn't even know she existed. I swear if I were older than twenty-two, I'd seriously consider a vasectomy. But, as it stands, Lily's pretty cool, and I may want to make her some siblings someday.

"Daddy, I have to pee again."

I sigh. Then again, I think I'll put that make-her-some-siblings plan on the back burner.

A few hours later we're in Ohio, cruising in our rental car, closing the gap between the airport and Chase's house.

Oh, hell.

With each passing minute, my stomach churns a little more. I know I'm a dick to thrust Lily on my brother unannounced. I can't worry about it now, though. We just drove through the little town of Harmony Creek and are nearing Chase's house.

"Are there really little kids like me where we're going?" Lily asks.

I glance back at her in the rearview mirror. She's in the car seat I remembered to buy and check with our other luggage at the airport. Lily is peering out the window at the verdant landscape. She must be mesmerized by all the gently rolling hills and sprawling farmland. Lily has only known the desert — brown terrain and cacti — so I'm sure she feels like she's on another planet right about now. Good thing she's young and adaptable.

"Yes," I reply. "There are two little kids at the house where we're going. I told you that already. Remember, I said Uncle Chase and Aunt Kay have children around your age."

"Uh-huh."

I've told Lily all about Jack and Sarah, repeatedly. She knows they're her cousins and she's excited to meet them. But she continues to question if they're really real.

That makes me wonder if Cassie was in the habit of telling Lily there'd be little kids at the places where she dropped her off, only to have our daughter discover she was stuck with adults.

"The kids will want to play with me?" she asks,

worried. "Oh, Daddy, I hope they like me."

Lily sounds so forlorn that something in me swells. I don't know how to explain it, but it's like my daughter's happiness is suddenly tied to *my* happiness. *Weird.* All I know is I really want Lily to feel accepted.

"I'm sure Jack and Sarah will like you just fine," I assure her, hoping that'll be true.

We reach the farmhouse just then, and I tamp down my own apprehension.

Here goes nothing…

The house looks the same as always, a three-story creamy white frame structure with slate-blue shutters, situated on acres and acres of land. There's a detached garage with an apartment above it across from the house, at the far end of the long driveway, and that's where I park the rental car.

"We here?" Lily wants to know.

I take a deep breath, exhale slowly. "Yeah, we're here."

The moment of truth has arrived. There's no more hiding from Chase why I'm really in Ohio.

I figure I probably have about five more minutes of peace before all hell breaks loose.

Or maybe less, seeing as Chase is already outside, walking over to the car, his gaze locked in on Lily.

Shit.

TEN

Will

"HOLD up, I can explain," I say to Chase as I slam the driver's door shut behind me.

"Oh, you better," he says.

Spinning away quickly, so I don't have to face my brother's penetrating steel-blue gaze, I open the back door and get to work on unbuckling Lily from her car seat.

Unfortunately, my fingers are shaky and I fumble with the straps, allowing Chase plenty of time to reach me.

He nudges me aside. "Here, I'll get that."

Mr. *I've-Been-A-Father-For-Six-Years-and-I-Am-A-Pro-At-This* has Lily out of the car seat in less than a minute.

"So, what's your name, sweetheart?" Chase asks Lily as he lifts her into his arms. He turns and shoots me a look that conveys I have *a lot* of explaining to do.

When Chase sets Lily down on the ground, she peers up at him and says, "My name's Lily."

"Lily, huh? That's a very pretty name."

Chase sounds distracted, and I can see he is assessing. That platinum-blonde hair is a tip-off, for sure, but it's the distinct green eye color that gives Lily away as being my child.

But if there was ever any doubt, it's blown away like a dynamite blast when Lily tells Chase, "My daddy says there are little kids here. Can I go play with them now?"

Remaining eerily calm, even as his eyes meet mine, Chase says, "Daddy, huh? Well, your *daddy* is right. I have a son and daughter of my own. Their names are Jack and Sarah, and I'm sure they'd love to play with you."

"Yay, yay!" Lily bounces up and down on her toes.

When we all turn to head over to the house, I notice Kay is out on the porch, watching our exchange. From the shocked look on her face, it's clear she's heard most of the conversation.

Chase takes Lily's hand and starts over to the porch, but not before turning to me and pointing. "Stay here," he tells me. "I have some questions for you."

Oh, I bet he does.

I shrug. "Okay, bro."

Kay takes Lily into the house, and Chase is back in no time at all. "Come on," he says. "Let's go someplace where we can talk privately."

He gestures to the detached garage with the apartment upstairs. Kay lived there once, before she and Chase hooked up.

With a resigned sigh, knowing I'm in for an epic lecture, I follow Chase up the wooden steps on the side of the building.

When we step inside to the bright galley kitchen, I remark, "Not much has changed up here."

The apartment was remodeled years ago by our father, and Chase has kept it up since. It's a great little space, cozy and neutrally decorated. There are cool skylights in the ceiling, fashionable furnishings strewn about, and fresh-smelling Berber carpeting that appears to be fairly new.

"You put that in recently?" I ask, nodding to the carpeted floor.

Chase seems in no mood to talk remodeling. In fact, he gets right to the point. "So, that little girl, Lily, is *your* daughter?"

Sighing, I run my hands through my hair. "Yeah. Yeah, she is."

"You sure, Will?" I give Chase a look, and he raises his hands. "I'm just looking out for you, baby bro."

He is. That's true, and I can't be mad he has my best interest at heart.

"How long have you known?" Chase asks. "Not for long, clearly, seeing that I sure as hell don't recall a little girl with blonde pigtails running around last weekend at your graduation ceremony."

I have to smile at that image. It would've been a trip for all involved. And, yeah, I did put Lily's hair in pigtails this morning before the flight. I looked up how to do it on Google and discovered it really wasn't all that hard.

Chase sees me smiling and prods, "Will?"

"Oh, yeah, sorry, I was lost in thought for a sec." I clear my throat. "To answer your question, I only found out about Lily, like, two days ago. Cassie is her mother, in case you're wondering."

"I figured that based on Lily's age." Chase snorts. "But how'd *you* end up with her? Cassie's just A-Okay with you taking her child to another state?"

"Uh, I don't think she cares one way or the other."

"What does that mean?" Chase looks worried now.

"Well," I breathe out. "Good ole Cassie paid me a visit late Thursday night. Guess she heard I was in town and decided it was finally time to let me know I've had a daughter for the past five years."

"Shit, Will."

"Oh, and there's more. She gave me Lily."

"*Gave* you Lily? Will, really, what the fuck does that mean?"

I lean forward and brace my elbows on the breakfast bar. Lowering my head to my hands, I say, "Cassie is a fucking mess, Chase. She's a total addict these days. I could tell she was high when she dropped Lily off. And she just pushed her on me. What was I supposed to do?"

I look up, and Chase is shaking his head. "Jesus."

"I know, right? I had no choice but to take Lily. I tried denying it to myself, but then I kept looking at her eyes." Chase nods, agreeing that the matching color is uncanny. "Even so," I continue, "I kind of panicked and asked a friend to rush a DNA test."

"And?"

"Lily is definitely mine, Chase."

"Does Mom know?"

"Hell, no!" I let out a snort. "And I don't intend to tell her, not yet anyway. She's on that extended vacation, so that's kind of good. I'll just deal with her when she gets back."

Chase is well-aware our mom is a spaz, so he doesn't argue with me on that point.

"So," he says slowly, "what are you planning to do now?"

"That's just it, man. I can't do this dad thing all on my own. I start that new job on Monday. And, I know nothing about kids." I wave my hand in the direction of the driveway. "You saw me down there by the car. It takes me ten minutes every damn time to get Lily in or out of that damn car seat. Every question I have on what to do with her I have to Google." I pause and rake my fingers through my hair. "Look, I'm sorry I didn't tell you ahead of time. I admit that was a shit move. But, Chase…" I trail off, swallowing the lump that's forming in my throat.

My brother places his hand on my shoulder. "Hey, you don't have to figure everything out today."

"Thanks, bro." I let out a breath. "I knew you'd understand."

Chase pulls me in for a hug and hell if I don't need one right about now.

"Hey," he says, patting me on the back. "Everything will work out. It always does, Will. I'm glad you came to me. We'll get through this together, as a family, okay?"

"I had nowhere else to turn," I admit, my voice catching.

"It'll be okay," Chase assures me as we break apart and step back. "But, for now, let's head on over to the house so I can get to know this little niece of mine."

ELEVEN

Will

CHASE grills up some burgers and Kay makes homemade French fries for dinner. Damn, those two sure know how to cook. I dig into the meal with enthusiasm, as does Lily.

I don't know, though. Jack and Sarah seem to pick at their food. And Kay and Chase take normal bites. Maybe Lily and I are just famished. After all, the past couple of days have been too hectic to eat a whole lot.

Sitting across from me at the dining room table, Lily talks little-kid shit with her cousins. She's not shy at all, lending further credence to Cassie's assertion that our daughter is used to new people. Knowing that makes me glad Lily is away from her mother. Having Lily around family is one thing, and totally acceptable, but passing her off to supposed "friends" — who are probably more like strangers or, worse yet, drug acquaintances — is flat-out asking for trouble.

For not the first time in the past two days, I'm happy Lily is with me. And that gets me to thinking that I may not want to leave Lily in Ohio for the *whole* summer. Chase and Kay have no idea I plan to leave her with them at all, though, so I guess I may as well bring the subject up while everyone's in a good mood.

"So..." I cough and clear my throat, garnering Kay and Chase's attention. "I think we should talk about some things I've been thinking about."

Chase eyes me warily. "Okay, shoot."

I place the last of a damn good juicy burger on my plate and wipe my mouth with a paper napkin.

"I've been considering my options," I begin. "And I think if I could leave Lily here for a couple of weeks, it might be enough time to secure some decent daycare for her up in New York City."

Lily, who up till this point has been preoccupied playing—along with Sarah and Jack—with French fries that they purposely dropped on the table, looks over at me sharply.

"Daddy's leaving me *here*?" she asks, her little voice stricken with panic.

Lily may be adjusting, and she seems to be getting along with Jack and Sarah well enough, but she clearly doesn't want me to abandon her, like her mother just did.

"It won't be for long, sweetheart," I try to reassure her.

That just makes tears well up in her eyes, and an empathetic Sarah pats Lily on the arm and tells her, "No be sad, Illy."

Jack leans in and I hear him whisper, "Don't worry. It'll be okay, Lily. We'll keep you company."

Great. I feel like an ass for bringing up the subject with the kids still seated at the table. I'm not the only one thinking it was a mistake. Kay winces at my blunder, and Chase just shakes his head and rolls his eyes at me.

"Why don't you kids go play upstairs," he says gently to the children.

Quietly—they can sense it's adult-talk time—Jack leads Sarah and Lily from the room.

When the kids are out of sight, Chase twists in his chair to face me. "So, Will." I can see he's losing patience with me. "How exactly do you see this going down? I mean, like, what's the long-range plan here? You didn't mention a word about leaving Lily when we were over at the apartment."

I throw up my hands. "Why the fuck do you think I came here?" I ask.

With his words clipped, Chase says, "Oh, I don't know. I guess I was stupid enough to think you wanted me and Kay to meet your daughter, who also happens to be *our* fucking niece."

Kay places her hand on Chase's arm. "Chase, please."

It's a plea for him to calm down. I know my brother's seething inside. I've pushed far too many buttons of his for too many years. I really can't blame him for his wariness now.

Sighing, Chase says, "Seriously, Will, you have to think this thing through. You can't leave that little girl here in Ohio. You think the best thing is for her to get used to being a part of our family for the next couple of weeks, maybe more, and then rip her away? Not to mention, she needs to spend time with you. Two days on the job doesn't make you a father, Will."

"Uh, um," I stammer. "I guess I haven't really thought it through."

"Obviously," Chase retorts.

He may be right, but his attitude still grates on my nerves. "Whatever," I mutter.

When I hear him mumbling back, "Typical," I lose my shit.

"I'm not asking *you* to watch Lily," I snap, pushing my chair back so that the legs scrape on the hardwood floor.

I'm feeling more trapped than ever now that I'm faced with the cold, hard truth.

"Look, Lily and I will just go," I say, standing abruptly. "You said you'd help, but that was obviously a lie."

"Quit being a hothead," Chase spits out.

"Oh, that's rich," I snap. "A hothead, huh? Guess *you* would know."

I turn, all set to storm out of the room, but then Kay chimes in with, "Will, please. Just sit back down so we can talk."

I reluctantly comply, since Kay is a sweetheart. "Okay, okay." I blow out a breath as I plop down on the chair I never pushed back in.

"Let's hear your plan," Kay says to me. And then, turning to Chase, she adds, "You have to admit Will's stuck between a rock and hard place, hon. I think we need to at least hear him out."

Chase, stubborn as he is, shrugs. "Yeah, sure, let's hear him out."

"Well," I begin, "I figured Kay's here every day with the kids anyway—"

Chase cuts me off. Pointing an accusatory finger my way, he says, "You are *not* pushing your responsibility off on my wife."

"I don't mind," Kay interjects. "It's only for a couple of weeks."

I have Kay on my side at the moment, and I throw in, "At the absolute most."

Chase still isn't thrilled, that much is clear from his sour expression, but before he can derail my plan, I suddenly remember how he and Kay once mentioned that a daycare recently opened down at the school where Kay used to teach first grade.

After downing a much-needed gulp of ice water, I say, "Hey, I have an idea. What if I enroll Lily for a couple of days each week at that daycare you told me about, the one down at Holy Trinity Elementary?"

Chase, who hasn't looked over at me since he got ticked off, finally meets my gaze. "Go on," he urges.

"Having Lily out of the house a couple of mornings would lighten the load on Kay, right? Plus, Lily would get used to hanging around kids other than Sarah and Jack. Maybe that'd make it easier for her to adjust when she has to leave."

"You don't have to enroll her in daycare," Kay murmurs.

But Chase overrides her when he says, "I think that'd be fair, for everyone involved."

My brother smiles over at his wife, like an "I just want what's best for you" assurance. When she smiles back, understanding and appreciation so clear on her face, I am struck with a feeling of longing for a bond like theirs.

Quit being a pussy, I chastise myself. Two damn days with Lily and I'm in some kind of weird nesting mode. Truly, I need to get the hell out of here. I need to haul my ass to New York, and start behaving like a man.

Yeah, leaving your kid behind is really manning up, dude.

Kay is speaking to me, not saying that of course, though she probably should. I mentally smack myself and whisk away all these stupid thoughts.

"You remember Emma Metzger, right?" Kay is asking me.

Oh, hell yes, I remember, but I carefully reply, "Hmm, not sure."

"Emma is Missy's cousin," Kay continues, clueless to the fact that I know exactly who she means. "And Emma recently took over my old teaching position. Anyway, she also runs the daycare down at the school. You'll need to talk with her, to see if she has a spot open for Lily. I'm sure she can fit her in. But, just to be sure, I'll give her a call tonight and bring her up to speed."

"Great, thanks," I murmur as I try to continue to play it cool.

Kay is persistent, though. "You sure you don't remember Emma?" she presses as she cocks her head, probably curious as to how I could forget Emma Metzger.

I'm trying to play it off, for my brother, who is watching my every reaction. I'm sure he's worried that if I'm still hot for Emma — which, if she looks as good as she did back when we were teens, I sure as hell will be — it'll somehow cause trouble. See, like Kay mentioned, Emma is Missy's cousin. And Missy is married to Chase's business partner, Nick Mercurio.

"Um, I don't think I remember her," I maintain, to keep up the farce.

Chase, as suspicious as Kay of my strangely foggy memory, says, "You met Emma at our wedding reception. Spent quite a bit of time with her, as I re—"

"That was, like, seven years ago, dude," I interject.

"You sat and talked with her half the night, Will."

"Yes," Kay chimes in, always supportive of Chase. "You two talked for hours. I remember you telling Emma about your plans for college, even. Chase and I were sitting at the same table for a while, that's how I know what you talked about. And, actually, now that I think on it further, I also remember you sharing how you were hoping to someday publish that comic book you were working on at the time."

Oh, yes, that one-time dream. Sighing, I push regret aside.

I better fess up, or this will get weird. "Oh, yeah," I say, like it just dawned on me who this girl is. "Emma Metzger, right. I remember her now. She was the girl with the long, silky black hair and the really blue eyes, right?

Kind of resembles Mila Kunis in the face?"

Emma was gorgeous back then. But there was more than that driving my attraction to her. She was cool, and we really hit it off that night. I talked with her for a long time, sharing things I only shared with Cassie at the time.

But then I fucked it all up.

At the end of the night, Emma asked me to walk with her out to Missy's car, so she could grab a hair tie or some shit. I knew it was her ploy to get us alone, which was fine with me.

Emma lingered at her cousin's car, even after she retrieved her hair-thingy. I thought she was so freaking beautiful. And her body was bangin', all perky tits and long-ass legs. I was so used to tiny Cassie, and here was this girl who could almost look me in the eye.

And she did exactly that.

I remember getting lost in her eyes, mesmerized by their varying shades of blue, churning and stormy, like the sea. I wanted to kiss her right then, hard and unyielding. And I knew she wanted me to make a move. After all, providing an opportunity to kiss was the real reason we'd snuck off to be alone.

But then I panicked.

I'd only ever been with Cassie at that time, even kissing-wise. Embarrassed, I ended up acting like the fifteen-year-old boy that I was.

There was Emma, giving me her best seductive "kiss me you idiot" look, and what did I do?

I stumbled back and told her, "We should probably go back inside. It is my brother's wedding reception, after all, and I don't want to be rude."

She blushed so deeply I actually watched her cheeks turn from pink to red, clear even in the dim glow of the street lamps.

"Yes, of course," she said.

Embarrassed — so embarrassed — she sounded absolutely mortified. At fifteen, there we stood, pretty much shattered — me by my own stupidity, and her, by me.

And I had no clue how to fix it.

"I'm sorry," I said in a rush. "I'm just not —"

" — that into me," she finished for me, brushing past me, all huffy. "No need to explain, Will."

"No, it's just… It's not that," I tried to explain. "That's not the reason at all."

I reached for her arm, to stop her from leaving, but she ducked away. "Leave me alone," she hissed.

"At least, let me walk you back inside," I begged.

She hesitated, but when I stepped toward her, she backed away and held up her hand. There were tears in her cat-like eyes. "Seriously, Will, just stay away from me, please."

"But —"

"Will…"

She choked back a sob, and I acquiesced. "Okay."

That was the last time I ever saw Emma Metzger. My few visits back to Harmony Creek since that day, I never bothered to look her up. First, there was Cassie to think of, and then I just got too busy with school.

But now I *have* to see Emma, to ask her if she'll watch my kid. A kid I didn't even know I had until three days ago. *Fuck. My. Life.*

Chase is eyeing me more suspiciously than ever now that I've grown so quiet. He knows something happened that night.

"Yeah, that would be Emma," he finally confirms, referring to my earlier question.

"This is so great," Kay innocently chimes in. "You two will have a chance to catch up."

Under his breath, Chase mutters, "Don't encourage

him."

"Dude." I roll my eyes at him.

What does he think happened that night? And what does he think I plan to do now? Hook up with Emma?

Truthfully, though, I wouldn't pass up a second chance with her. Like I said, she was hot back then, and I'm sure she's even hotter all grown up. She must be. Chase wouldn't be so worried about me making a move on her if she wasn't still cute.

My expression betrays me and Chase kicks my foot under the table. "Just behave, Will. Don't forget Missy is her cousin, and Missy's husband is my business partner."

Ah, see, the underlying *real* reason why Chase is wary of my intentions.

I put up my hands, in an effort to placate him. "Okay, okay. I got it. No working my smooth moves on Missy's cousin."

Chase completely misses my attempt at a joke, but Kay, to her credit, gets my humor and smiles over at me.

Something is clearly still worrying Chase, so I ask, "Hey, what's up your ass?"

"I'm just thinking about Lily," he responds.

Instantly defensive, I say, "I thought we had this all worked out? I swear I'll be back in two weeks, max, to pick her up."

Blowing out a breath, Chase says, "So, that's how you plan to work it?"

"What do you mean?" I am truly stumped as to where this is heading.

"Well, Lily is obviously too young to fly alone. I thought maybe you'd ask me and Kay to drive her up, but it sounds like you're coming back to pick her up, yeah?"

"Yes, Chase. I'm coming back to pick her up." I resist the urge to roll my eyes.

And then my brother finally gets to what's really

bugging him. "And how exactly is that supposed to work? You don't have a car, Will. The one outside is just a rental."

"Uh, yeah, that one's a rental, but…"

Chase doesn't know about the extravagant graduation gift — the BMW — my mom gave to me, but he must suspect something. *Shit*.

"Will?" Chase prompts.

"Okay, yeah, I have a car. I already set it up to have it driven from Vegas to New York next week."

Chase is well-aware our mom likes to spoil me, and, in a quiet voice, he asks, "Is this the graduation gift Mom was being all sly about last weekend?"

I blow out a breath. "Yeah, it is."

"So, what'd she get you?"

"A BMW convertible."

Chase runs a hand over his face. Leaning back, he mutters, "Unbelievable."

My brother isn't jealous or anything like that. He just hates that our mom substitutes material things for actually being there for us. He does have a point; it is a pretty fucked-up situation.

Kay places a hand on Chase's arm, the one with the words *I stand before you, judge me not* tattooed around his bicep. I stare at his ink and think how — on this day — those words apply more to me than to him. 'Cause here I am, standing before my brother, asking him for help, since frankly I am floundering.

"Bro," I say quietly.

Chase looks over at me, and I clear my throat. I want to be as honest as possible, just to lay the facts on the line.

"Look, I know I'm asking a lot with all of this. But, seriously, it isn't just for me. I'm asking for Lily, too. I just want to do the best thing for her, I really do."

Chase nods, accepting me at my word. Kay also smiles over at me encouragingly.

But me? What's going through my head?

Well, truth be told, I can't shake the feeling that if I really wanted to do the right thing for Lily, I wouldn't be leaving her at all.

TWELVE

Will

THE next morning, Chase and Kay rope me into going to church with the family.

As I let out a groan, Kay tells me, "Emma will be there. After mass, you can talk with her about enrolling Lily in daycare."

"Oh, joy," I reply. I was planning on just calling Emma, but my fate appears to be sealed.

I spend the next half an hour putting on a suit and helping Lily into her fancy duds. Well, the suit part takes all of five minutes, maybe seven with tying the tie. Lily is the problem-dresser.

While throwing frilly lavender fabric in my face, she crosses her arms over her undershirt-covered chest. I got that on her at least, along with a pair of lavender leggings. It's the dress that goes over everything that Lily doesn't like.

"I go like this," she declares, pushing out her bottom

lip.

My patience is worn thin this morning. "Lily, just put on the goddamn dress."

"Quit swearing!" Lily chastises, and rightly so.

"I'm sorry, Lil," I say, humbled by my five-year-old.

My daughter finally allows me to slip the dress over her head. But as I'm helping her put on her shiny patent leather purple shoes, I know something has to be brewing in that little head of hers. She's far too complacent suddenly.

A few minutes later, when we head out to Chase and Kay's minivan, parked in the driveway, I realize why. Seems my tattle-tell daughter can't wait to run up to Chase and inform him, "Daddy swore. And it's not the first time, either. It's just awful, Uncle Chase. He has potty-mouth."

Chase breaks out in a devious smile. "Hmm, that *is* awful, Lily. Potty-mouth, huh?"

"Uh-huh."

"Don't worry, sweetheart. I'll make sure your daddy receives a suitable punishment for his terrible language."

"This from Mr. Gutter Mouth," I grumble under my breath as Kay takes Lily and helps her get settled in the minivan.

When Kay slides the door shut, she gives us a look. "Brothers," she says, shaking her head and walking away.

Chase places his hand on my back and urges me to, "Come on, get in," as he slides open the minivan door Kay just shut.

I balk. Lily, Jack, and Sarah are all buckled in their car seats, but they're still hyper as hell, bouncing around everywhere. These kids are far too lively for the early morning hour.

"You expect me to sit in the back with all the kids?" I glance over at the rental car. "I think I'll just follow you to church."

Chase gives me a shove. "No, we're already running

late. Just get in the back. There's no room for you up front."

Now I know what Chase meant when he told Lily I'd receive a "suitable punishment" for swearing in front of her.

"You're such an asshole, dude," I whisper, so the kids don't hear me swear again.

As I reluctantly crawl into the only open space, the seat next to Lily, I hear Chase laughing.

"I'm glad this is so amusing for you, Chase. Just wait. I'll think of some way to get you back. And when I do..."

Chase appears not to be one bit worried. "Yeah, good luck with that," he tells me as he slides the door closed in my face.

Just as I'm conjuring up ideas to make my big bro pay, Lily reaches over and takes my hand. It's the sweetest gesture, something simple and pure. And with that, I abandon all plans to get Chase back, because I then realize that putting me in the back with the kids was never meant as a punishment. Sitting next to my little girl, her hand secured in mine, is truly a gift.

THIRTEEN

Emma

WILL Gartner. What a dick. Okay, not really. But I need to tell myself that or I'll succumb to his charm, like I did back when I was fifteen years old.

I put myself out there, made a move so we could be alone at that stupid wedding reception. And what happened? Will didn't *want* to kiss me, despite the fact I practically threw myself at him. *Ugh.* I'd never felt more unattractive in my life. Will Gartner was gorgeous — probably still is — and he shut me down.

Nonetheless, for some inexplicable reason, I've thought about him often since then. I guess there was just something about him, a crazy, but undeniable, connection that I haven't felt since then…with anyone. There was no one like Will at college, and certainly not anyone like him here in Harmony Creek.

Do connections like that stand the test of time, though?

Guess I'll find out soon enough, seeing as Will is back in Harmony Creek, with a kid this time. He apparently has a daughter named Lily, who he didn't know existed until three days ago.

Kay filled me in with an overview of the situation last night when she called. She was somewhat cagey on the details, but I understood why. She wants to try to paint her brother-in-law in the best light.

Still, the facts are the facts. Will got some girl pregnant back when he was sixteen, probably a result of a one-night stand. Let's face it, a guy as devastatingly handsome as Will surely has — and had — girls throwing themselves at him. Hell, even teenage-me wanted him. Though, in my innocence, I was only hoping for a kiss.

Now that I think on it, no wonder Will rejected me. I must've seemed so pathetic to him, batting my eyelashes, trying to flirt in my teen-girl naïve style. What a fool I was.

And why should now be any different? I'm still not exactly Miss Experienced.

Out behind the school, I kneel down by a flower bed I am slowly filling with beautiful blooms. Frustrated by all this thinking about Will, I grind the trowel I've been holding deeper in the dirt.

With that task completed, I set the little shovel down, and then loosen the roots on a small impatiens plant. At last, I plop the tiny flower into the hole I've created.

I'm strategically hidden from view of the churchgoers this morning, on purpose. Once Kay filled me in on what was happening, that Will wanted to talk to me after church about putting his daughter in my daycare program, I decided to skip mass.

Truth is I'm just not ready to see Will.

I mean, what if I'm still interested in him? Based on the fact he never once tried to reach out to me during any of his prior visits to Ohio — though, in his defense, they were few and far between — I can only assume he's forgotten all about me.

So why can't I forget about him?

How do men even do that — get under your skin and stay there for ages?

Focus on the flowers, Emma.

Father Maridale, my boss, has been bugging me to plant flowers behind the school. And luckily the greenhouse was opened bright and early this morning. I stopped by and purchased four flats of impatiens, in varying colors, that were just screaming for a home in the flower beds. The plants I'm working with at the moment have coral blooms.

But I'm running out of coral, which means a flat of white impatiens is in order, to add a contrasting row.

Crap. I couldn't carry all the flowers to the back of the school, so if I want white impatiens, it's going to require a dash to my car.

I stand and smooth back strands of raven hair that have fallen from my long ponytail. It's then I notice how filthy my hands have become. "Yuck," I mutter.

I'm probably sporting nice dirt smudges on my cheeks, too.

Oh well, I don't plan on running into anyone, I remind myself.

Still, just in case, I wipe the rest of the dirt from my hands down the sides of my faded jean shorts. And then I hurry over to where I parked my car, around the far side of the building, away from prying eyes.

At my Mini Cooper, I grab the flat filled with white impatiens from the backseat, and then bop back over to the flower bed as quickly as I can.

But then . . . "Damn."

As I round the side of the building, I see I'm about to be discovered, and by the one person I've been hoping to avoid for a little while longer.

Yep, the good-looking guy, standing with his hands in the pant pockets of what appears to be a well-tailored suit, and seemingly assessing my work in the flower bed, is none other than Will Gartner.

And, dammit, he still gives me butterflies in my stomach. "Why?" I groan.

He must hear my lamenting, since he spins around to face me. "Emma?" he says, lifting what I hope is an appreciative brow as he scans me from head to toe.

When he stops to linger on my bare legs, I return the favor and ogle him.

Will Gartner is as hot as ever—maybe hotter. He's taller than I remember, over six feet for sure. And those shoulders, they're broader than before. *Wow.* Will sure did grow up. He's clearly all man these days, and Lord help me, I'm more smitten than ever.

"Hi, Will," I squeak out.

Striking green eyes that melted me seven years ago crinkle at the edges as he smiles over at me.

He takes a step toward me...and then another. I can tell as he nears that he's still checking me out, though he's trying to be sly about it.

I don't care. Truth is, I love the attention, *his* attention. A traitorous part of me—my libido that's screaming for me to acknowledge that I'm more insanely attracted to Will than ever—applauds me for wearing super-short shorts and a cute navy V-neck tee that's tight in all the right places.

Was I subconsciously hoping to run into Will today, despite my sorry attempt to avoid him? Yeah, I probably was.

I suddenly remember the flowers in my hands and hastily set the flat on the ground.

"It's good to see you again," Will says, his voice far

smoother and more confident than I remember.

"It's been a long time," I murmur, wiping my hands down the sides of my shorts. Why do they feel so sweaty suddenly?

"It has," he agrees.

Our eyes meet, and I know he's remembering that night at the wedding reception, so long ago. Is that regret I see? Does he wish he'd kissed me way back then? The fire's still there, that's for sure.

I suddenly want Will to kiss me, right here, right now. But that'd be ridiculous, right?

Tearing my gaze from what must be the most hypnotizing eyes, like, *ever*, I say softly, "It's nice to see you again, too."

Lame, but it's not a lie. As much as I was hoping I wouldn't still feel so strongly about Will, I'm kind of glad I do. Because he makes me feel...

What?

So damn *alive*, that's what. And that strong wave of emotion, and tingling excitement, is exactly what I liked about him all those years ago, and also the reason why I was so appalled when he rejected me.

Would he reject me today, though?

So much has changed; we're no longer bumbling teens.

I smile over at him. He smiles right the hell back, warming me in places other than my heart, and I conclude: *I don't think he would reject me, not today.*

Enough, though! Really, this is crazy. But is anything ever sensible when lust is involved?

"So"—I clear my throat, refocusing on why Will actually sought me out—"I heard you wanted to talk to me."

"Yeah, yeah, I do." He takes a step back suddenly, like he needs some space to think more clearly.

Good, I want to affect him like he affects me.

"It's about my daughter, Lily," he continues. "She's going to be staying with Chase and Kay for a couple of weeks, while I get settled in New York City. I thought maybe she could spend a couple of mornings each week at the daycare. You know, to give Kay a break and all."

Whoa, wait. I'm suddenly very annoyed with Will. When I was seven my father left one day, just up and took off, out of the blue. I later learned he ran off with a woman he'd been having a long-term affair with. In any case, the specifics don't matter. What matters is he never came back. And to this day, he barely keeps in touch with me.

How freaking abandoned I felt back then.

Wait, check that. I *still* feel abandoned by that jerk. Fifteen years have passed, and his leaving still stings.

Those dredged-up emotions make me empathize with Lily, and I say, voice tight, "How old is Lily, anyway? Five, right?"

Will nods slowly, like he's not sure what's causing this suddenly cool attitude of mine. "Yeah, she's five," he confirms.

Shaking my head disapprovingly, I tell him, "You shouldn't leave her, Will. Didn't you just recently discover she's yours?"

Now a little cool himself, he says, "Sounds like Kay told you everything."

Hands on my hips, I reply, "Not everything, but enough. Don't be mad at her, though. You think word of Lily won't get out around here?" I let out a scoffing noise. "We're a small town, Will. Everyone finds out everything, eventually."

"Clearly," he says, his tone thick with irritation.

I'm getting to him. Good.

"Anyway," I continue, "what I'm trying to say is that two weeks are bound to feel like two *months* to a little kid. And what if it takes you longer than a couple of weeks to get things set up?"

I can tell I've hit a nerve. Will looks guilty as hell, like maybe he *was* thinking of dragging out his time away from Lily.

He runs his fingers through his light brown hair, and I wish it didn't look so soft and silky, so inviting. "I don't plan on leaving my daughter here in Harmony Creek indefinitely," he says quietly.

"Still, it's unfair to her."

His brow furrows. He's probably wondering why I'm so passionate about a little girl I've never met. And, really, what the hell *am* I doing?

Before he can ask why I'm going off like this, I swish my hand in the air. "You know what? Never mind. I have no right to question you like this."

"Hey, it's okay," he says. "It's a good quality to have, putting kids first, especially when you run a daycare."

He's trying to be nice, even after I've been such a bitch.

Softening my demeanor, I revisit his reason for seeking me out in the first place. "What days were you thinking of signing Lily up for daycare?"

He looks relieved to get back to business. "Would Tuesdays and Thursdays be okay? Like, just in the mornings. Would that work?"

"Yeah, that's not a problem."

"Okay, then," he says. "I'll tell Kay to bring Lily in on those days."

I nod.

Will appears torn on whether to stay or go, but he eventually says, "I guess I better go."

He starts to walk away, but I don't want him to leave, not like this. Seeing each other for the first time after all these years shouldn't end all icy and up in the air.

Why does everything between us always have to feel so, well, unfinished?

"Hey, Will."

He spins around. "Yeah?"

I take three steps toward him, narrowing the gap, and he cocks a brow.

Reaching for his arm, then re-thinking and dropping my hand back down to my side, I release a breath. "Look, I'm sorry. Really, I am. I didn't mean to jump all over you before."

I almost confess everything right there. How I purposely tried to avoid this meeting with him, how I still feel kind of embarrassed over our non-kissing incident all those years ago. How I think he's one of the best-looking guys I've ever met, how I wish I wasn't still so insanely attracted to him, and how he makes me crazy with all these conflicting feelings.

But before I get out a single word, Will reaches out and cups my face in one large hand.

I'm rendered speechless, immobile. Ooh, his touch feels *nice*. But what the heck is he doing?

Gently, he moves the pad of his thumb over my cheek. "There's a tiny dab of dirt right here," he whispers as he swipes it away softly. "It's been driving me crazy." He chuckles and brings his free hand to my other cheek. "And there's another smudge over here."

With my face in his hands, I peer into his emerald-green eyes. "Will," I whisper.

"Emma," he says softly, and then, "Look, I made a stupid mistake all those years ago. We were just kids..."

He trails off, and I realize we are practically pressed against one another. "Just kids," I murmur as I close my eyes. "But we're not kids anymore, are we?"

"No, we're not." His warm breaths are a gentle caress as he lowers his lips to mine. "Maybe it's time we make things right?"

"Mmm, yeah, maybe it is."

I am so ready for this kiss. I don't care that we're on church grounds, in the back of the school. I don't care I was just irritated with him, and I don't care he confuses the hell out of me. This kiss is seven damn years in the making. And I just know it's going to be so good.

But then, just as our lips are about to touch, a little voice filled with curiosity rings out, "Daddy, whatcha doin'?"

FOURTEEN

Will

I AM generally not this assuming or forward, but damn, Emma looks so good. And the connection is still there. There's this pull I can't deny, a gravitational force that's compelling me to just go for it and kiss her.

For this one awesome moment, I feel like we're the only two people left on the planet—the last man and the last woman. But that couldn't be further from the truth, which I'm reminded of just as I'm about to right a seven-year wrong.

Lily's little voice shatters the illusion and sends me straight back to reality, as I hear, "Daddy, whatcha doin'?"

Emma and I jump away from one another like we've been caught doing something bad. Kissing isn't bad, though, right? I don't know, 'cause when I turn to face my daughter, I feel so busted.

How can such a tiny little person dole out such a look of consternation? Or is that curiosity? My kid-radar isn't too finely honed yet.

"What're you doing, Daddy?" Lily repeats, much more softly this time, like she knows she's interrupted something meant for adults.

"Nothing, sweetheart," I reply. "I was just talking with Miss Metzger."

I look past Lily, but see no signs of Chase. He, Lil, and I walked over to the school after church when I noticed Emma's car parked off to the side of the building. Chase was supposed to wait out front with Lily, while I spoke with Emma in the back. Kay had abandoned us by that point, having taken their kids to the minivan shortly before mass ended when Jack starting acting up.

"Where's Uncle Chase?" I ask Lily.

She points to around the side of the school. "He on his way. We coming to see why you take so long to come back." Lily giggles, and then adds, "I run *way* ahead of Uncle Chase, though."

Crouching down, I beckon her to come over to where Emma and I are standing. A respectable distance from one another, I might add. "Come on over, sweetheart. I want to introduce you to someone really nice."

Tentatively, Lily approaches. She tucks her chin in as she walks and by the time she reaches me, her eyes are glued to the ground.

I introduce her to Emma, and she looks up curiously.

"Miss Metzger runs the daycare," I say. "It's this really fun place where kids can play with other children. And you know what?"

"What?"

"I was just talking with her, and I think I fixed it so you can hang out there a couple of mornings each week, while Daddy's up in New York. Doesn't that sound like fun?"

Lily nods. "Uh-huh." Glancing up at Emma, she adds, "You know my daddy?"

Emma smiles down at us both. "Yes, honey, I know your dad."

She was about to know me better, till Lil interrupted.

My daughter's curious gaze jumps from Emma to me, and then back to Emma. "My daddy likes you, doesn't he?"

"Uh…"

Emma blushes, looking far too cute for words, and I suppress a chuckle.

Lily is not deterred. "Daddy was giving you a kiss, like he gives me. I saw him."

"Uh, it's not exactly like that," Emma mumbles, her cheeks turning from pale pink to flaming red.

Not only is Emma cute, she's fucking hot. I probably shouldn't have tried to kiss her back here behind the school, but it felt so damn right.

While Emma fumbles around nervously, shifting from one sneakered foot to the other, I save her from further embarrassment by answering Lily's question. "Yes, Lily, Daddy likes Emma. But in a very different way than how Daddy cares for you."

I leave it at that. After all, Lily *is* only five.

"Okay," she mumbles, already losing interest in the subject.

"Hey." I stand, hoisting my daughter up to my hip in the process. "What do you think is taking Uncle Chase so long to catch up?"

Just then my brother rounds the corner, looking completely exasperated. "Sorry," he says. "I had to detour over to the minivan. Jack was starting to give Kay a hard time again. He's more than a handful this morning."

"No problem," I tell him.

Chase nods a hello to Emma. "Hey."

She gives him a little wave. "Hi, Chase."

Jack was great on the way to church, but he grew restless

during mass. The kid has a lot of energy, reminding me of how Chase and I were when we were kids.

With that thought in mind, I say, "Girls seem so much easier," Giving Lily a squeeze, I add, "Isn't that right, Lil?"

I receive no reply, as Lily has fallen asleep. Her arms are draped loosely around my neck, and her head rests on my shoulder, her thumb in her mouth.

God, she's a doll.

Chase jerks his chin to Lily's sleeping form and agrees. "Girls sure are much easier. Sarah's out, too. Just like Lily."

Emma makes a scoffing sound. "You two are just too funny. Wait till your girls are teenagers. I bet they both give you a run for your money. Oh, and would I love to be there when they bring home their first boyfriends."

I clutch my daughter protectively. "Hey, there will be no boyfriends for Lily for a long, long time."

"Sarah's not dating till she's thirty," Chase chimes in nonchalantly, like this is just a given fact.

Emma laughs. "Ha, *riiight.* I'm sure your girls might have something to say about those silly rules."

"Silly?" Chase scoffs. "I think not."

"I'm with you, bro," I'm quick to add.

My brother and I bump fists, and Emma rolls her eyes at our shenanigans. After a few additional parting words, Chase and I leave Emma to her gardening and head over to the minivan.

On the way, with Lily sleeping in my arms, I lean down and sniff her hair. The kid always smells so good to me.

Chase raises a brow and asks me, "You sure you want to leave tonight?"

I let out a groan. The truth is I don't want to leave Lily, not really. My heart is telling me to stay, but my head makes me say to Chase, "I have to go, bro. I can't blow this new position. It's everything I've ever dreamed about."

Is it, though? I ask myself. My real dream has always

been to strike out on my own, freelance my graphic skills, get that comic book published as a graphic novel.

Chase knows all this, and he knows *me*, so it's no huge surprise when he says, "If the big city and the corporate fast track are what you really want, Will. Well, then I say go for it. But if you ever change your mind and decide to follow a different path, just know I'll support you in any way I can."

I look over at my brother. He's thirty-one now, but you'd never know it. He looks pretty much the same as he did at twenty-five, except for a few small laugh lines around his eyes. But that's okay. Those lines are a subtle reminder that Chase's life is happy and exactly the way he wants it.

He followed his heart and found his way.

Maybe I should take a page from my brother's book and do the same.

FIFTEEN

Will

WHEN we return to the house, I lay a still-sleeping Lily down in her bed in Sarah's room. I then head to the bedroom I've been staying in.

I really need to think things over.

Easing down into a chair by the window, my suit still on, and the blinds closed on the sunny day outside, I place my head in my hands and mull over my options.

But then I realize there's no mulling to be done. My fate was sealed the moment Lily came into my life. I just couldn't see it clearly until today.

I can't leave Lily, not this soon. We're only just now getting to know one another. And sure, she'll be with me again once I set up child care for her in New York, but it won't be like this. I'll be working all the time. We need more time, so that when I do leave, it won't be so traumatic for her.

With Emma's concerns still banging around in my

head, I conclude that staying with Lily, for now, even if it's only for a few more days, is the best thing to do.

Decision made, I contact the service scheduled to drive my car to New York this week. I inform them that there's been a change in plans, and promptly ask, "Can you drop my car off in Ohio, instead?"

I learn that, for a price, everything can be adjusted.

"For a small up-charge, your BMW can be in Harmony Creek by Wednesday night," I am told.

"Great," I reply as I approve the extra fee.

I then call the corporate recruiter who hired me, so I can tell him I can't start the new job tomorrow. He's not happy, but he makes a few calls and gets back to me within the hour.

"The best I could do is a one-week reprieve," he tells me. "But, you absolutely *must* be in New York City, ready to start work, next Monday. Another delay like this, Will, and you'll lose this opportunity."

"Okay, got it."

My head is back in my hands. *I hope I'm not fucking things up too badly.*

I head downstairs and inform Chase and Kay of my plans to stay an extra week. They are thrilled. And then I go tell Lily her daddy isn't leaving tonight, after all. To say she is over-the-moon happy would be a severe understatement.

"It's only for a few extra days," I carefully add, to prepare her for my imminent departure. "We *will* have to be apart for a short while after that."

"Why?" Sad green eyes implore me.

"Lil, I'm still going to need to get things ready for you up in New York," I explain. "It shouldn't take long, though, I promise."

Lily loses interest in explanations quickly, and this time is no exception.

Wrapping her little arms around me, she tells me, "Okay, Daddy. But when you go, you come back fast as you can, okay? You're more fun than Mommy."

I'm taken aback. This is the first Lily has mentioned her mother since day one. I've come to the conclusion, though, that Cassie was more like a big sister to Lily. She was always pushing her off on other people, like her daughter was a bother. In addition, Lily's easy acceptance of staying with me leads me to conclude that Cassie spent very little time overall with our daughter.

Well, I won't abandon Lily. I plan to be a great father to her.

Still, I decide to stick with the Tuesday and Thursday morning daycare plan, knowing it'll be good for Lily to grow accustomed to a structured environment. That'll be her life in New York, after all. Plus, like I told Chase and Kay, she'll have a chance to interact with kids other than Jack and Sarah. Those three get along well, but there are occasional scuffles.

An added advantage to the daycare plan is it gives me an excuse to see Emma again.

What can I say? The girl has me intrigued, and I really want to kiss her, at least once, before I go.

On Tuesday morning, when I take Lily to daycare, I have my first opportunity to take steps toward making that elusive kiss happen. I purposely leave early and reach the school before any other parents or kids arrive.

A light rain is falling, and since I forgot to bring umbrellas, Lily and I have no choice but to make a run for the school.

"This is fun," Lily tells me as she jumps in all the puddles on the way to the entrance.

"I'm glad I remembered your boots." I say, nodding to her bright yellow galoshes.

"Good call, Daddy," she says, making me laugh.

Lily heard Chase use that exact phrase last night, but it sounds so funny coming out of her mouth.

As we near the entrance, we spy Emma unlocking the school doors. She appears fully focused on her task, and mischievous Lily whispers to me, "She don't see us, Daddy. Let's sneak up on her."

"Okay," I agree, knowing that when Emma sees me she's *really* going to be surprised. "This should be fun," I add.

Lily and I go into ninja-mode, moving stealthily. We reach the protective overhang unnoticed, and then sneak up behind Emma, who remains oblivious.

Oblivious, that is, till Lily screeches out an enthusiastic, "Boo!"

Startled, Emma spins around till she's facing me and Lily.

"Lily," she breathes out, hand on her heart. "And... wait. Will?"

"We scare you," Lily says, giggling.

"Yes, you sure did," Emma confirms. Her gaze flitters back to me. "And Will, seeing you here is even more of a surprise."

"I bet," I reply.

"So, what happened?" Emma says, just as she's reaching up to push back her hair.

Her raincoat gapes open, and my eyes are immediately drawn to the hot little purple dress hiding under her coat. It's not anything overly skimpy, but the clingy fabric hugs her lean curves in all the right ways.

Tearing my appreciative gaze away, I start to straighten Lily's askew pink backpack, simply as a ruse to hopefully detract from my blatant ogling.

"Well," I reply nonchalantly, glancing up at Emma. "I guess you could say there was a slight change in plans."

Emma is trying to hide the blossoming smile on her

lips. "Clearly," she says.

Hmm, does that sly grin mean she's happy I stayed, or is she simply glad for Lily's sake?

"Miss Met-ger," Lily interjects, tugging Emma's raincoat sleeve. "Daddy says I get to stay with you today."

In a voice used with little kids, Emma peers down at Lily and says, "Yes, you sure do, Lily. And I, for one, can't wait. I have lots of fun things planned for you kids to do today."

"Coloring?" Lily wants to know.

"Yes. And drawing and games. Does that sound good to you, Lily?" Emma inquires.

My daughter nods. "Yes, Miss Met-ger."

"Hey, you know what?" Emma places her hand sweetly on Lily's shoulder. "You can just call me Miss Emma if you want."

"Okay, Miss Emma"

Squeezing Lily's shoulder lightly, Emma says, "You sure look pretty for your first day."

I appreciate what Emma is doing—bonding with Lily so she'll feel comfortable when I leave her for the morning. I also feel a moment of dad pride that Emma noticed Lily's outfit. Yeah, that's right—I'm not a total misfit of a father. I managed to dress Lily in one of her prettiest outfits, a snow-white dress with a red roses print. Lil was also patient enough this morning for me to brush out her hair, leaving her platinum locks shiny.

"What do you say?" I prompt Lily.

"Thank you," Lily says as she flips her glossy hair back over a shoulder. My daughter is such a girl already.

Lily's cuteness doesn't go unnoticed by Emma, and we share a smile.

Turning back to the door, Emma pushes, but the rain seems to have made it stick. And, hell, I am only too happy to help out.

Taking over, I prop the door open with my body and beckon for Emma and Lily to go in the school.

Once we're all standing in the front hallway, Emma turns to me and Lil and says, "Since you guys are a little early I can show you the daycare area, if you'd like. Lily can pick ahead of time which table she'd like to sit at."

"Sounds good," I reply.

But just as I'm about to take Lily's hand and follow Emma, the wall across from us garners my full attention. Or rather, the giant mural Chase and I painted on that wall several years ago, back when I was fifteen, has me faltering.

"Wow," I murmur. "I can't believe this thing is still here."

Lily stares up at me curiously, and Emma comes to stand by my side.

With my eyes glued to the wall, I explain why I'm so taken aback.

Pointing to the mural, I say, "My brother and I painted that scene one summer when I was staying with him. Wow, it sure was a *long* time ago, though."

I smile as I recall the hot summer day when Chase and I created the art in front of us now—a scene of a cartoon kid walking along a trail, on his way to a bright red schoolhouse. Cute and cuddly cartoon forest creatures cheer him on as he makes his way under a bright blue sky.

"It really is adorable," Emma says. Her own eyes are now fixed to the wall. "I admire it every time I come into the school." She places a finger on her lips, contemplative-like. "For some reason, though, I always thought Chase painted the mural by himself. I guess since he's touched it up a few times over the years."

The colors appear to be a bit faded, so I say, "Looks like it could use some re-touching again."

"Yeah," Emma says on a sigh. "Chase hasn't done

anything with it for a long while."

"Yeah, well, he's been really busy with work," I say, in way of explanation. "His business keeps growing and growing."

My eyes return to the mural, and I step closer to what was once my and my brother's giant canvas. I touch a faded brown squirrel that conjures so many memories, and softly murmur, "This is the first thing I painted on the day we started the project."

Lily comes over to the wall and touches the foot of the squirrel. That's about as high as she can reach. "You color this, Daddy?" she asks.

I hoist her up on my hip so she has a better view. "Not just colored, Lil. I painted it, too."

"All by yourself?" she wants to know.

"Not all by myself, no. Your Uncle Chase painted the sky… and the trees…." I move her to the different sections so she can reach out and touch every part of the painting.

Some of the animals are more faded than others, and paint is chipping away from parts of the sky. No doubt about it, the mural could definitely use some touching up.

And, suddenly, I have an idea.

Turning to Emma with Lily in my arms, I contain the smile that's fighting to break free, and say, "Hey, I was just thinking. Maybe I can come in and touch up the mural."

"That sounds great!" Emma proclaims.

And then she's smiling, and I'm smiling, and everything's great.

"Good," I say. "It's a plan, then. Let's see… I have this whole week off before I head up to New York, so—"

"Wait." Emma looks confused. "I thought you were staying in Harmony Creek?"

Aw, crap, another miscommunication. Will we ever be on the same page?

"Not permanently, Emma. The position in New York is

still a go. I was able to delay my start date for one week, so I can spend more time with Lily, but I still have to leave."

Emma's face falls, her disappointment palpable. "Oh, I just thought...something different."

"Anyway," I say, veering back to the subject of the mural. "Maybe I can come in this week and touch up some of the faded parts."

"I help color, too?" Lily wants to know.

"Sure," I say. I suppose I could let her paint something.

Emma huffs. She seems upset with me, but why? Why does she care so much that I'm leaving?

"You'll have to do it during an evening," she snaps coolly. "You can't be here disrupting the kids."

"What's dis-rup-ing?" Lily asks.

Setting my daughter down, I say, "I'll tell you later, Lil."

I turn and face Emma. "Evenings are fine," I say tightly.

I want to ask what her deal is. Why is she so damn hot and cold with me? I sense she's attracted to me, as I am with her, so what's the problem? Sure, I'm leaving, but it's not like I'll never see her again. Hell, we almost kissed the other day, and she sure wasn't pushing me away then.

Women, I swear.

I search for answers in Emma's blues, but find nothing.

"Will," she says on a sigh. "Maybe we should sit down and talk things through sometime."

"I'd like that," I say. "Since, frankly, I think I'm as confused as you seem to be."

"It's just..." she trails off, begins again, "It's complicated, is all."

"It doesn't have to be, Emma."

I'm ready to sort this thing through right the fuck now, but Emma gestures to outside the doors, where other parents are beginning to show up with their kids. "You better go, Will. Now's not the time to get into a big discussion."

With the new arrivals delayed with lowering their umbrellas outside the doors, I say in a rush, "What about tonight? You have plans?"

She looks surprised. "Um, yeah," she says. "I'm busy."

"What about tomorrow, then? We could go out to dinner. That would give us a chance to talk."

And maybe you can finally enlighten me as to what the hell is bothering you, I think, but don't add.

"I'm working," Emma replies.

I sigh. "I meant at night."

"Oh."

"Well?"

"Will."

"Emma."

"Okay, but it's not a date."

"Fine, it's not a date."

Ten minutes later, after saying good-bye to *go-with-the-flow-I'll-be-fine-Daddy* Lily, I'm walking out of the school, thinking the whole time that Emma Metzger may not see our upcoming dinner as a date, but I sure as hell do.

SIXTEEN

Emma

"WHAT the hell did I agree to?" I ask Missy as I hop around my small but very messy apartment.

I'm trying to find the matching black pump to the one on my left foot, and I've just about torn up the place in my quest. While I hobble around, tossing around clothes and such, Missy contents herself with lounging around on the sofa.

Admiring her freshly painted nails, she says, "You agreed to go out with the unbelievably hot Will Gartner." And then, with a wistful sigh, she adds, "That kid sure has grown into one fine man."

"You're not helping," I say dryly as I drop to the floor to continue my search on my knees. "I am so doomed."

"Oh, Emma, it's no big deal," I hear Missy murmuring as I peer under an easy chair in the corner of the room.

I stop what I'm doing and glare up at Missy like she's

lost her mind. "Ah, I beg to differ, cousin-dear. This *is* a big deal…to me. I mean, why go out with Will when he's leaving in less than a week? I am so stupid." I resume my search for the lost shoe, muttering, "I never should have agreed."

Thirty seconds later, Missy is tapping me on the shoulder. "Here." She hands me the rogue pump. "I found your missing shoe."

"Huh." I stand up and slip it on my stockinged foot. "Where'd you find it?"

Missy points to the sofa to where she was just sitting. "It was in that mess you created," she says, gesturing to a crumpled throw and a pile of clothes.

"Wow, I really have made a mess of things," I mutter.

"Hey." She squeezes my shoulder. "About Will…"

"Yes" — I sigh — "about Will."

"Just have fun tonight, okay? You deserve a nice dinner with a good-looking guy like him." She sighs. "Just don't go messing things up, like I did way back when with Chase. Play it cool, Emma. Don't give in to that damn Gartner charm."

"Ha, that's easier said than done."

"For real," Missy agrees, blowing out a breath.

Missy has a history with Chase. Their encounter happened long before Missy married Chase's business partner, Nick Mercurio, though. It also occurred before Chase knew Kay. Nonetheless, for a long time afterward, Missy lusted hard after Chase. Understandable, since he is really hot, just like his younger brother.

Clearing her throat, and mercifully changing the subject, Missy says, "So, those shoes really match your dress perfectly, don't they?"

"They do," I agree as I straighten the hem of the black lacy dress I have on. I motion for Missy to follow me into my bedroom. "Hey, come on in and talk with me while I finish my hair. The flat iron should be hot by now."

At the doorway, Missy leans on the jamb while I get to work on straightening my naturally wavy hair.

Eyeing me curiously, she asks, "So, why *did* you agree to go out with Will? I mean, apart from the fact that he is a stunning specimen of man that would be hard for any woman to resist."

I lower the flat iron to my side and come clean. "Truth is, I really like him, Missy, more than I should." Our eyes meet in the mirror. "That's the problem, too. I don't *want* to like him."

"Why? Is it only because he's leaving?"

"Well, yeah, there is that. But I also think it's screwed up he can't commit to his daughter."

Missy shrugs. "I don't know how true that statement is, hon. Kay tells me Will is great with Lily."

I resume working with the flat iron, and Missy comes in the room and sits on the edge of my bed.

After a minute, I dismally declare, "Anyone can be great with their kid when it's only for a week."

"It's not just for a week, Emma. Will's taking Lily with him to New York, right?"

I bark out a laugh. "Yeah, but not till he basically has round-the-clock daycare set up for the kid. I don't know about you, but I sure don't call that being committed." Sighing, I add, "I hate to imagine what he'd be like in a relationship, seeing as even his daughter has a lower priority than his precious career path."

In a soft voice, Missy says, "Do you think maybe you're seeing a little too much of yourself in Lily?"

I set the iron down with a clatter. "She's five years old, Missy!"

"And you were seven when your dad left."

Missy's hit a nerve, but I try to stay calm and reasonable. "Look," I say, "I don't deny I have abandonment issues.

But this situation with Will, it's not just that. Sometimes, he just...really...irks me."

Missy eyes me knowingly. "That's because you're really into him."

"And there it is, we've come full circle," I admit with a groan.

Missy shoots me a small commiserating smile. Every woman knows that feeling of misplaced affection, the one where you pretty much have to give in, because fighting is useless.

With my hands covering my face, I mumble through my fingers, "Ugh, you're so right. God help me, but the truth is I really do want to start something with Will."

Yes, God help me indeed.

SEVENTEEN

Will

I DON'T plan to tell Chase I'm going out on a date with Emma. I suspect he wouldn't approve of a) me going out on *any* date when I'm leaving in four days, and b) me going out with Emma, specifically.

Dressed casually in jeans and a navy button-down shirt, I jog down the stairs to find Chase and Kay in their living room, watching TV.

I stick my head in the room and say, "Hey, guys, I have a few errands to run in town. Can you keep an eye on Lily while I'm gone?"

They agree without questioning me, so I get the hell out of the house before they figure out I'm being less than forthcoming.

In my car—the BMW that arrived a few hours ago—I call Emma.

Still set on not calling this what it is, a date, she refuses to let me pick her up. "I'll just meet you at the restaurant," she tells me.

She's stubborn, but I kind of like it.

When I arrive at the bistro, I have the hostess lead me to a quiet table in the back. Before she leaves, I ask her to let Emma know I'm here already.

When the waiter comes around for the third time, ten minutes have passed. Emma is late, so I go ahead and order a bottle of wine.

Emma arrives, finally, just as the wine shows up.

"Ooh, going all out for our non-date, I see." She nods to the bottle.

There's teasing in her tone, and a smile playing at her lips, so I know she's not mad.

"I hope you like pinot grigio," I reply.

"Love it," she says as she sits down in the chair across from me.

Damn, she looks good. For someone who claims this isn't a date, she sure has dressed like it is. Not that I'm complaining. In those sleek heels, her long legs seem to go on forever. I can't help but imagine how much better they'd look wrapped around me if we were to ever —

"Will, hey. Earth to Will." Emma waves her hand in front of my face. "Thought I lost you for a minute there."

Clearing my throat, I compose myself and reply in my smoothest tone, "No, no, I'm here. I promise you, Emma, I am one hundred percent in this moment."

I smile over at her, and she smiles back. And soon, things begin to feel more right for me than they have in a long time. There's something more than lust between Emma and me, something I can't define. I don't know what it is, but it feels...potential.

Too bad I'm leaving on Sunday.

Dinner comes and goes, and we order a second bottle of wine. I end up drinking far more than Emma. It feels good, though, to let go. I've been under a lot of stress lately.

As my inhibitions fall away, I flat-out ask Emma, "So, what is it about me you don't like?"

She switched over to ice water a minute ago and is in the process of taking a drink. Or, rather, trying to, as my question catches her off guard and she coughs and sputters.

"I like you," she says, setting her glass on the table and wiping her mouth with a cloth napkin.

"Eh." I shrug. "You say that, and I *feel* like you do, but there's something bothering you." I wave my hand around, like I'm swishing away this undisclosed something between us. "I feel it, Emma, your hesitation. That's why you didn't want to call this a date, right? Something about me bugs you, doesn't it?"

"Jeez, Will, nothing like getting right to the point there."

I lean back in my chair. "Seriously, Emma, just tell me. I'm a big boy, I can take it."

She doesn't look so sure.

Eyeing me warily, she says, "I just feel bad for Lily, that's all."

"Okaaay…" I pour the last of the wine into my glass and take a long sip. And then, since I'm thoroughly irritated now, I throw her earlier words back at her. "Jeez, Emma, nothing like getting right to the point there."

I glare over at her. She can't maintain the intense eye contact for more than a few seconds, and, looking down at the table, she murmurs, "You asked me to tell you what's been bothering me."

"Yeah, I did." I sigh. "But I'm trying to be a good father to Lily. It's unfair to expect me to be perfect. Let's not forget, this is all new to me. Her mother dumped her on me unexpectedly. Hell, up until last week, I didn't even know I had a kid."

She shakes her head, like she's trying to rid herself of

some bad thought. "I know all that, but…"

"What? Just spit it out, Emma."

And then she does. "I'm not questioning your intent, Will. But you're still leaving Lily —"

"And like the plan before," I interject, "it's only for a couple of weeks, max."

"And then what?" Her blue eyes flash with fire, telling me someone left this girl once and that's really why she's mad. "What kind of life is Lily going to have in New York with you working all the time? She's never going to see you. I bet when it gets really tough, you'll send her back to her mom."

I snort. "That is *never* going to happen. I don't even know how to reach Cassie."

"See," Emma says, pointing at me accusingly. "That's exactly what I mean. You'd consider it, wouldn't you? You'd give up Lily if you knew where Cassie was."

She has me all off-track now, and the wine clouding my brain isn't helping matters. Would I give Lily back to Cassie? I don't know. Not if Cassie's still using, no way. But if she were clean…?

"I don't know what I'd do," I admit.

Instead of blowing up at me, like I fully expect her to, Emma says softly, "You can't just give her away, Will. That's the same thing as leaving her. Lily needs her father. Daughters need their dads."

Emma reaches over and snatches my glass of wine. She takes a sip, and then sets the glass down, her fingers wrapped tightly around the stem. "I'm sorry," she says, eyes downcast.

I reach over and gently pry her fingers from the wine glass before she snaps the stem in two.

"Hey," I say quietly. "Is this really about Lily? Or is this about you?"

She then tells me about how her dad left her family

when she was only a couple years older than what Lily is now. She explains how it made her feel, how it *still* makes her feel.

"It's irrational, I know. But I'm glad I came clean with you. I'm sorry, but I can't help the way I feel, Will."

"I'd never do that to Lily, though," I adamantly declare. "Even if Cassie took her back, I'd always stay in her life."

Emma scoffs. "Yeah, like that'd work out, with you in New York and her out west."

Now, I just want to leave. I motion for the waiter to bring the check and when he does I throw a bunch of bills on the table. "Let's get out of here," I say, my words clipped.

"I'm sorry I ruined our date," Emma murmurs as we head for the door.

"It wasn't a date, remember?"

I don't know why I'm suddenly being a dick. Or maybe I do. The conversation we just had has hit a little too close to home, making me realize I'm only partially committed to keeping Lily with me indefinitely.

As we near where the cars are parked, Emma says, "Hey, Will. Let me drive you home. You had a lot more to drink than I did."

I consider it, since I am a little more than buzzed. "What about my car, though?" I motion to my shiny BMW.

Emma's eyes widen when she realizes what kind of car I have. "Wow," she murmurs. "What happened to the rental?"

I lean against the side of my car. "The rental company came to the house and picked it up."

"And this one is yours?"

"Yep."

She shakes her head, and I swear I hear her mumble something about the "different worlds" we live in. Maybe she's right.

Fishing the keys from my pocket, I say, "Hey, I'll see you around."

Before I can go, though, Emma places her hand on my arm. "Will, wait. Seriously, you shouldn't drive. I'm sure Chase or Kay can bring you back tomorrow to pick up your car."

She does have a point, on all counts. "Okay," I reluctantly agree. "I guess you're right. Though I don't think my brother is going to be happy when he finds out I was out with you."

She laughs as we walk over to her car. *Great, a Mini Cooper. This is going to be far from comfortable for someone tall like me.*

"Oh, really," she replies. "Why would Chase be mad we went out?"

Since I'm a little drunk, I don't sugarcoat the truth. "He's worried I'll take advantage of you."

Opening the passenger side door for me, she says, "That's sweet of him, but I think I can take care of myself."

I can't argue with that; she certainly put me in my place tonight. Or at least gave me a lot to think about. My respect for Emma has gone way up. She's not some pushover I can take advantage of, and I like that about her.

Once we're in the car, but before we back out of the parking space, she looks over at me and asks, "What are you thinking, Will?"

Again, I say the first thing that comes to mind. "I'm thinking that I really like you, Emma. I like you a lot."

With clear regret in her tone, she says, "I kind of like you, too, Will."

"Why do you sound so sad about it?" I ask.

"Because you're leaving in a few days, remember?"

"Ah, yes, there is that."

We drive to the house in silence, but with my head full of thoughts. Thoughts of whether I should stay in

Harmony Creek and pursue my dreams of freelancing, and thoughts of whether it's wise to pursue Emma any longer, since I *am* leaving in a few days. But most of all, above everything, my main concern is what's really, truly best for Lily.

Because one thing for sure—I don't ever want her to feel the way Emma does—abandoned by her father.

EIGHTEEN

Will

I DON'T try to kiss Emma when she drops me off at the farmhouse. There's a moment, though, where she hesitates, and I think she may want me to.

But really, what's the point? Like she said, I'm leaving in four days.

"Hey, thanks for the lift," I mumble as I slip from the car, which actually turned out to be roomier than I had expected.

"No problem," she replies quietly.

She sounds disappointed. Did she *expect* me to kiss her? Oh, well. I don't want to make out with her while half-drunk anyway. If I ever do kiss Emma Metzger, it will be with a clear head.

With my hand on the top of the open car door, I lean in and say, "Guess I'll see you tomorrow when I drop Lily off at daycare."

She nods, but doesn't make eye contact. "Guess so."

I tap the top of the door twice, consider saying more. But in the end, I just close the damn thing and walk away.

I linger, however, in the driveway, watching Emma's headlights grow smaller and smaller as she backs down to the road. When she's out of sight, I sigh, wishing our situation was different.

But it's not.

Inside, the first thing I do is check in on Lily. As usual, she's in Sarah's bedroom with Sarah. Both girls are sound asleep in beds I assume Kay has pushed together for the night. I give both Lily and my niece kisses on their forehead, noting how Sarah resembles Lily a lot. Her hair's not blonde, though, like Lil's. Sarah's is the same chestnut shade as Kay's.

Leaving the girls, but not before making sure the nightlight is on, I head down the hall to my bedroom.

My room is located next to Chase and Kay's bedroom, and I stop in the hall and consider knocking on their door to see if Chase is still awake. I really feel like talking to him. Maybe he can help me sort out all my confused thoughts. My brother's usually good at that sort of thing.

But, just as I'm about to rap on the door, I hear murmurs and soft gasps from the other side. I lower my hand. Chase is clearly preoccupied with his wife, so I shelve that idea.

In my own bedroom, loneliness overcomes me. I find myself thinking of Emma again. If she were here, one thing is sure—I'd make her feel amazing, like Chase is apparently doing with Kay in the room next to mine.

I wonder if there'll be any girls like Emma in New York City. Probably not, I conclude. Emma is small-town, but in a good way. She's not pretentious or snobby. She doesn't even care that I have money—thanks to Greg and my mom, of course. That leads me to think about how I'll be making my own bank soon enough. That prospect is what attracted me to the fancy ad firm I'll be working for in the first place — the lure of a big paycheck.

"Yeah, you'll be living the dream soon enough," I murmur to my drunk-ass self.

Too bad I'm not inebriated enough to forget that the life I'm about to embark on is not the one I really want at all.

NINETEEN

Will

THEY say moments of clarity come at the strangest times, most often when unexpected.

My moment of clarity regarding Lily occurs exactly like that, at 8:05 on a Friday night, as I'm down at the school, watching in awe as my "who knew she was *this* insanely talented" daughter paints a perfect rendering of a little brown squirrel, directly below the large one I finished touching up minutes before.

My daughter is wildly gifted. She is, and it finally sinks in.

Emma is standing next to me, facing the mural, and sharing the moment with me. There's something very right about that.

Emma arrived unexpectedly, shortly after Lily and I started painting. She claimed she'd forgotten something at the school. *Yeah, right.* She knew Lily and I'd be painting here tonight. The real tip-off to her cute ruse is that she hasn't made a single move to retrieve her supposedly left-behind item.

I suspect Emma Metzger secretly wanted to see what Lily and I were up to. Or maybe she wanted to see *me*? In any case, I'm happy she's here. Especially to share in this special moment, this act of discovering my daughter is beyond gifted.

We watch Lil go to town, and, damn, I can't believe the diminutive five-year-old little girl making art before my eyes belongs to me.

A wobbly, "Wow," is all I can manage to croak out.

"Maybe Lily is a prodigy," Emma whispers as she leans in to me.

I like this closeness, and I revel in it as I move closer still and whisper back, "Lily likes to doodle in her coloring books. I mean, I see her sketching crap all the time. But I don't think I've *ever* seen her draw anything quite as good as this." I gesture to where Lily diligently works on her squirrel. "*This* is something special, Emma."

"It is exceptionally good for a five-year-old," Emma agrees.

"Hell, it'd be pretty damn good for a *twenty*-five-year old," I retort.

"It would be, Will, it really would."

"I guess I should probably start paying more attention to what Lily is working on in those coloring books."

"You *should* pay more attention, Will," Emma replies.

Whoa, that comment is laden with hidden meaning.

"Don't worry," I reply, chuckling, "I plan to."

After a few more minutes of watching Lily, who is now deeply engrossed in getting the squirrel's tail just right, Emma says, "Well, you and Chase are really talented at art, so this shouldn't come as a complete surprise."

I let out a snort. "We weren't good like *this* till we were way older."

"Hmm, looks like the artistic gene must be extra strong in Lily."

"You're not kidding."

And then Emma says something that gives me pause. "At least with you parenting her, she'll have a chance to develop her talent. I'll be sure to encourage her to draw a lot at daycare the next couple of weeks while you're gone."

"Thanks," I murmur.

I feel shitty. Emma is really starting to care for Lily. This isn't some girl just working my daughter to get close to me. Emma is a genuinely good person. She'll make a good mom someday, I have no doubt.

Speaking of parenting, am I really going to be that much better of a parent than Cassie? I mean, sure, I don't have a drug problem, but with my upcoming schedule Lily will most likely spend as much time with other people as she was doing with Cassie. Better people, not druggies, but still essentially strangers.

I sigh, and Emma wants to know, "What's wrong?"

I shake my head, torn between what my heart still screams every day for me to do—stay here where my family is—versus what my head is now shouting, which is *get your ass to New York.*

"I just..." I falter, rake my fingers through my hair, and then begin again. "I'm just worried about when Lily comes up to New York. It's not like I'm going to have tons of time to spend with her."

"So, stay here in Harmony Creek."

"It's not that simple, Emma."

She steps away, putting some space between us. "The job in New York is not the only job in the world, Will."

"It's a good job, Emma."

She raises an eyebrow. "By good, you mean it pays a lot, right?"

"Whatever. I don't have time for this." I start to walk

away, to head over to the mural where I can escape an uncomfortable discussion, but Emma steps directly in front of me, blocking my path.

I roll my eyes. "I can just walk around you, you know."

"So, go ahead." Her lips press together and her ice-blue eyes dare me to move. "Walk away, Will," she hisses, low so Lily can't hear. "It seems you have that move down pat."

I stay right where I am, simply to prove her wrong.

After an epic stare-down, Emma's gaze softens. She touches my arm. "Hey, listen, I'm sorry. I'm really not trying to be a bitch."

"You're not a bitch," I assure her.

It's true. A bitch wouldn't be this concerned for Lily, or for me.

Emma releases a breath, and softly, again so Lily can't hear, she says to me, "I think you have the potential to be a great dad. And it's clear you love Lily already —"

"I do."

"— but I think you need to get your priorities straight."

"Wow, don't hold anything back."

She ignores my sarcasm. "I'm almost done, Will. But one more thing…"

"Yeah? What's that?"

"Please, before you leave, look inside your heart."

"Who says I haven't?"

"That's just it." Her tone is pained, almost pleading. "I think you have, a lot. And I think you're torn on this job in New York," — *wow, she nailed it* — "I also have a feeling it's not just because Lily has come into your life."

"Go on," I urge when it looks like she might clam up.

"Search in here, Will." She taps my chest, and it takes all my strength not to snatch up her hand and pull her to me. I've never wanted to kiss someone as much as I want to kiss her right now, this girl who sees into my soul. "Ask yourself what you want out of life. You're at a crossroads. Search, though, and you'll *know* what's right for Lily…and what's right for you, Will."

If only it were that simple.

The next morning, I awake with a start. It's nearly dawn and the rising sun is trickling through the window in dappled rays of filmy gold.

I haven't slept well at all. Emma's words have been haunting me, fucking with me ever since we parted last night.

After our discussion, I didn't have much of a chance to search my heart. What I really wanted to do was talk more with Emma, about lots of things. That girl challenges me, but she also sort of soothes me. In a weird way, she gives me focus.

But further conversation was not to be. Lily was hungry, and when we left the school Emma and I took her out for her favorite food—pizza. At the restaurant, we mainly listened to Lily chatter on and on about how fun it was to paint the squirrel on the wall.

"I made it look just like Daddy's," she said, filling me with pride.

"Yes, you did, Lily," Emma agreed.

And then Lily turned to me and asked, "Can we paint a squirrel like that on Uncle Chase's wall when we get home?"

"Umm…" I suppressed a laugh as I sat there imagining Chase's face if he were to come home and find a squirrel painted on his living room wall. Gently, I broke the bad news to Lil. "That's probably not a good idea, doll."

Lily took the letdown well, and the rest of the evening

was great. I feel like I really got to know Emma a lot better, especially when Lily slipped out of the booth to go play the claw machine.

I gave her a pile of quarters, and though the game was only a few feet away, well within my sightline, I still felt compelled to say, "Don't wander off, Lily. You stay right in front of that machine where I can see you, okay?"

"Okay, Daddy," she said with a huff as she walked away.

One minute later, Lily was pushing buttons, trying in vain to maneuver the crane behind the glass so the claw could hopefully pick up a stuffed animal.

"So, alone at last." I reached over and placed my hand over Emma's, and we fell into a discussion about our college days. Emma told me how she chose to major in elementary education since she loves kids so much.

When she let it slip that she hoped to have a family of her own someday, she made a face and was quick to add, "Not anytime soon or anything."

I knew she was concerned I'd read more into her comment, but I didn't, not at all.

"Yeah," I replied, sighing. "It'd be cool to have another little Lil someday. But, like, definitely way, way, way" — I made a huge flourish with my hand — "in the future."

Emma started to say something, but faltered. Instead of saying anything more, she stared down at her half-eaten slice of pizza.

"What is it?" I asked.

She glanced up at me, biting her lip. "Are you mad at Cassie for keeping Lily from you when she was a baby?"

I thought about it, then replied, "If you'd asked me that same question last week even, I would've said thank God she didn't tell me. But now…" I rubbed a hand down my face. "Ugh. Yeah, now I wish I'd known. I feel like I probably missed so much."

"Oh, Will." Emma met my gaze, her eyes so blue and so full of empathy.

I wanted to say more, much more, and I think she did too, but just then Lily skipped back over to the table and the moment was lost.

The night ended, and we parted ways. I knew I still had a lot to think about. I mean, I still needed to "search my heart," as Emma had suggested. But, by the time I finally got Lily to bed, I was too exhausted to think about anything. My head hit the pillow, and I was out.

Until the restlessness kicked in, restlessness that lasted throughout the night. And into this morning.

Flipping over to my stomach, I search now, asking myself: *What is best for Lily…and for me?*

Well, if I stay in Harmony Creek I can kiss the job in New York good-bye. Since Lily got cheated in the mom department, she deserves a successful dad, right? But does a little girl really care about material success? Something tells me Lily would rather have a dad who's present in her life than some guy who only has ten minutes here and there to spare. When I start that job in New York, that's about all the time I'll have for my daughter.

I prop up on one hand and punch the pillow with the other. Then, I roll over on my side.

At that exact moment, I hear the door behind me creaking open slowly. A tiny voice then squeaks out a tentative "Daddy?"

I roll over so I'm facing the door. "Lily?"

With the dim morning glow illuminating my daughter, I can see she's holding one hand over her mouth, like she might be hurt.

"What the…?"

I am up and out of that bed in three seconds flat.

Kneeling before her, I ask, "What happened, sweetheart? Are you hurt?"

She shakes her head and slowly lowers her hand from her mouth. I check her over but don't see anything wrong. The early morning light coming through the window, however, is not quite bright enough for me to say for sure.

I reach over and turn on a lamp. "Let me see your mouth, Lil."

Instead of giving me a good view of her face, Lily peers down at the hand that wasn't covering her mouth. It's clenched in a tight fist.

Now I'm really confused, until Lily opens her hand and I see what's in her palm.

"Holy shit, you lost a tooth!"

"Shit," Lily echoes.

I don't correct her for swearing. It's my fault I uttered the word in the first place. I really need to watch my language around Lily.

Nudging her chin, I urge her to look up at me. "Let me see which tooth you lost."

She opens her mouth wide and lowers her chin to reveal a gap on the bottom row.

"Cool," I murmur.

She closes her mouth. "You're not mad at me, Daddy?"

"Of course not, princess." I laugh. "Why would I be mad?"

"'Cause I make it happen. Jack tell me keep wiggling it...and I did. But, I didn't mean to break it, Daddy, I swear."

Tears fill Lily's eyes, and I pull her in for a big hug. "Aw, Lil, you didn't break anything. Your tooth would've fallen out no matter what you did or didn't do. You're supposed to lose your baby teeth, sweetheart"

"Why?" she murmurs into my shoulder.

"It's all part of growing up. And you know what?"

"What?"

"Someday you'll have all new teeth, grown-up teeth.

Doesn't that sound awesome?"

"Uh-huh."

"Jack has probably lost a few teeth of his own. That's why he told you to wiggle your loose one."

I lean back and ask to again see the tooth that fell out.

Lily hands it to me and I tell her, "You know what happens next, right?"

She shakes her head. "No."

As if this is the most serious of business, I say, "We have to put this tooth under your pillow tonight."

"Now?" she asks.

"Well, no, not now." I thumb over to the light coming through the window, which is growing brighter by the minute. "It's almost time to get up. We'll put your tooth under your pillow *tonight* when you go to bed. And then the tooth fairy will come and leave you money."

My daughter's eyes widen. "Really? No way!"

I nod. "Yes way. You'll find what he or she left you in the morning when you wake up. Money will be under your pillow where your tooth was. Cool, huh?"

"Guess so."

Her face falls, and I ask, "What's wrong?"

Sad green eyes meet mine. "You won't be here to see what the tooth fairy leaves me."

She's right. I couldn't secure a late-day flight out of Ohio. My plane takes off early Sunday morning. *Very* early.

But you don't have to be on it, a little inner voice reminds me.

And there it is, right there — my answer. My heart has revealed, right here and now, what is the right course of action. It didn't take searching to find the answer I needed, it just took Lily losing a tooth.

Everything is so clear now as I decide to stay right here with my daughter. I've already missed Lily's birth, her days as a baby, and so much more, I'm sure. I can't miss any more important events, like losing a first tooth. Those kinds of things occur only once in a lifetime.

I feel good, my decision to stay made. I'll deal with the fallout later, but for now, I am at total peace.

Most importantly, though, the happiness I feel when I inform Lily I'll be staying with her, and the gorgeous smile she gives me in return, is absolutely priceless. No job in the world could ever beat that.

TWENTY

Emma

S UNDAY arrives, and I assume Will has left for New York City. It's surprising to me that I've heard nothing from him since Friday night. It's a shame too, really. I had so much fun hanging out with him and Lily at the school. And then afterward, when we went out for pizza, I thought we'd really connected.

So, why has there been no text or phone call from him?

We never even had a chance to say good-bye, for heaven's sake. It's not like Will and I were dating, but still…

Men. They can be such thoughtless jerks sometimes.

That evening, in my distress, I call Missy and tell her everything. "Do you think I should text him?" I inquire when I finish my woeful tale. "You know, to see how his flight to New York went?"

It's a desperate move, and Missy calls me out on it. "Don't run after him, Emma." She sighs, knowing all too well the heartache we women sometimes have to endure. "Men do things according to a whole different schedule than us. Your two days without hearing from him probably feels like two minutes to him."

"Apparently," I scoff.

"Just let him call you, okay?"

Sighing, I get to what's really bugging me.

"I wouldn't care so much, Missy, if he hadn't been leaving. But not calling...or texting...or saying good-bye in any way." I exhale loudly. "I just don't know. Maybe something happened, right?"

"Emma." Her tone is a warning.

I know my cousin has my best interest at heart, but my own heart wants something completely different. "What if he doesn't call, like, ever again?"

"Then let him go."

The regret I feel makes me wish I'd done things differently on our last night together. "I never did get to kiss him," I lament.

Missy sighs. She thinks I'm being ridiculous, and maybe I am. But one thing's for sure — I won't allow myself to be in this position of *what-ifs* next time around.

"I'm telling you now, Missy," I proclaim, ready to back up my thought.

"What's that, hon?"

"If I ever have a second chance with Will, I'm going for it. No more holding back, in any way. I'm tired of waiting for things to happen in my life."

Oh, jeez, and if she only knew the half of it.

I vow then and there not to mess up a second chance with Will. I plan to kiss him, and to let him take my v —

"Emma, listen..." Missy trails off, distracted, as her kids begin arguing in the background.

She then has to hang up.

An hour later, I'm hanging out on the sofa, clad in

skimpy sleep shorts and a hot pink cropped tee. It's warm in the apartment on this muggy summer evening and the less clothes, the better. I grab a handful of chips from a crumpled bag sitting next to me and stuff them in my mouth.

Yes, this is my sad attempt to drown out all thoughts of Will Gartner. Reality TV and potato chips seem to be doing the trick.

I finish off the bag, and then run to the bathroom to pee and brush my teeth. Returning to the sofa to resume watching Kim and Khloe argue about something, as sisters are known to do, I am suddenly startled by a knock on my apartment door.

"Huh?"

I'm not expecting any guests since it is well after nine on a Sunday night. Who knows, though? Maybe Missy got the kids settled and decided to stop by to cheer me up?

I get up off the sofa and walk over to peer through the peephole....and...well. "Oh, shit. It's Will."

My thoughts are everywhere, all at once.

What's Will doing here?

Coming to see you, obviously, you fool.

But...but...why isn't he in New York? He should be there by now, right?

Who the hell cares?! Let him in!

I'm about to burst with joy that Will's still in town, but I won't allow such a thing till I find out why. Deciding the best course of action is to play it cool, for now, I open the door a small crack, effectively keeping my skimpily clad body hidden.

"Hello, Will," I say tightly. "Imagine seeing you here."

He shoots me one of his boyishly handsome smiles. *No, don't do that.* "Yes, imagine."

Don't let him woo you so easily, girl.

Since I never told Will where my apartment was located,

and random small talk should do the trick of making me appear blasé, I say, "So, how'd you know where I live?"

"I asked Kay."

"Oh."

So much for that diversion tactic.

Will folds his arms across his broad chest, making the navy tee he has on stretch tightly across his solid pecs.

Why the hell must he look so good?

Swallowing the appreciative sigh that threatens to reveal me, I blurt out in a rush of words, "Uh, I'm sorry, but I just can't do this. I thought you'd be up in New York by now. Did you change your flight or something? Was there a delay?"

"Not exactly," he says slowly.

When he peers past me into the apartment, I realize how rude it is to keep him standing outside. "Oh, do you want to come in?"

"Sure."

I open the door the whole way so he can come in, but he falters as he's afforded a clear, unobstructed view of what I'm wearing. Or, rather, how little I'm wearing.

His hungry gaze travels up my bare legs and exposed midriff, warming me in all the right ways.

Damn, no more pretending. I want Will as much as he seems to want me. And the dynamite between us is threatening to explode.

Clearing my throat, I say, "So, about New York…"

"I didn't go. And that's why I'm here. I want to talk to you about something, Emma."

I can't resist a touch of smart-assery, especially since I'm still not sure what, besides our insane chemistry, is going on with us.

"What exactly do you want to talk about? Did you feel the need to come all the way over to my apartment to tell me you missed your flight or something?"

With a chuckle, he replies, "I didn't miss my flight. This visit is about a little more than that."

"Oh, it is, is it?" I cross my arms and jut out my hip, making my short tee ride up even higher.

Will swallows hard, and I am eternally grateful for hot summer nights and the need for barely-there sleepwear.

He has to look away, and the raw emotion in his tone is clear when he says, "The truth is I came over here tonight to ask you for a second chance."

"A second chance?"

"Yes, with us. I've been thinking a lot lately, and I truly believe we should give this thing between us a real shot. Let's see where we can go with this. What do you say?"

He's so gorgeous, and the sincerity in his voice is endearing. I can't in good conscience keep up my charade of not caring.

"I'd like that, Will," I softly admit. I take a step toward him and add, "Does this mean you're staying?"

Tearing his gaze away from my body, he says gruffly, "Yeah, it looks like I'll be hanging around for quite some time."

"Well, that's good for Lily." *And for me*, I think, but don't add.

He glances at me, but quickly looks away. "It is," he says.

The sexual tension between us is unfathomable. Will staying in Harmony Creek is a game-changer. It's that second chance I wanted, an opportunity to do things differently with him.

Go for it, every fiber in my being prods.

Will rakes his fingers through his hair, mussing it up further. It's grown since he first came to Harmony Creek, and I like it all tousled as it is. It gives him a more carefree vibe, making him seem, well, more *him*.

I chew at my bottom lip, contemplating. Will always

looks amazing, but tonight he's working something more than his gorgeous face and hot body.

What, though? What's different?

Suddenly, I realize what it is. Will is unburdened and, dare I say, happy. He clearly searched his heart and made the right decision, for Lily *and* for himself. This unmistakable vibe makes me want to go to him, to somehow share in this palpable joy. And why shouldn't I? What I told Missy is true—I'm done holding back. I want Will, in every way.

And since he's staying...

With a raised brow, I coyly ask. "Do you have anywhere you need to be? Like, are there any other girls you have to deliver this good news to?"

Will laughs. "No other girls, I swear."

"Well, that's a promising start."

He closes the gap between us and wrapping his arms around me, he murmurs, "*This* is what I call a promising start."

And, finally, finally, finally, his lips crash into mine.

TWENTY-ONE

Will

W<small>E'RE</small> starting something here, and we both know it. The burn between us that's been simmering since I returned, a burn that ignited that long-ago night when I failed to kiss Emma, has finally boiled over.

And neither of us has the power to stop it. Not anymore.

With my hands wrapped in Emma's shiny raven hair, my lips find hers.

Finally.

She tastes like cherries and vanilla and, fuck, this may be the best first kiss ever. I think for her too, based on her enthusiasm.

She parts my lips and my tongue finds hers, both of us wanting more, more, more.

"We should slow down," she gasps when we come up for air.

"Yeah," I agree.

But when our eyes meet, what little resolve we may

have had goes straight out the window.

Three more minutes of non-stop kissing, and I am backing her toward the sofa.

"Not here," she gasps between kisses.

"Okay." It takes all I have to pull back. "Where, then?"

"In there." She points toward what I assume is her bedroom, and then our mouths are on each other once more.

I am *starving* for this woman.

Somehow, we make it to her bed. And then my hands are up that damn cropped tee that's been taunting me since I arrived at her apartment.

I sigh, "Emma," as I fondle her perfect, palm-sized breasts.

She is soft and warm, and I want her like nothing else. And when I feel her tugging down the zipper of my jeans, I know this is it. There will be no going back.

For a brief few seconds, I consider whether we should stop. I'm sure sex means a lot to a girl like Emma. But when her hand wraps around my bare cock, it's too late.

I… am… gone.

TWENTY–TWO

Emma

Is this is a mistake? I don't know. The way Will kisses me sure doesn't *feel* like a mistake. I want him, and that's all I care about right now.

In my bedroom, I make my intentions clear. I have Will gasping and falling back on the bed when I start sliding his jeans down his legs. He helps me get them to his ankles, and I quickly get to work on his length. First with my hands, and then with my mouth.

"Fuck, Emma," I hear him say from above me.

I know he's watching, so I flip my hair over my shoulder so he can see everything. When he's practically throbbing, I release him and move up his body, sliding his tee along his smooth chest as I go, kissing every inch of newly exposed skin.

Will shudders in delight, but then he sits up quickly and pulls his shirt over his head. Two seconds later, his jeans and boxer briefs join the tee on the floor, and this glorious man is naked in my bed.

"Wow, Will."

He lies down and pulls me on top of him. "What?" he asks.

He's grinning, and I'm certain he knows what I'm about to say. "You have the hottest body," I tell him.

It's true. He does have an amazing physique. Will is lean and cut, and I just want to lick him all over.

"You do?" He cocks a brow.

Burying my head against his smooth, hard chest, I mumble, "I can't believe I actually said that out loud."

He rolls me over onto my back.

Hovering above me, he whispers, "Don't worry. The feeling's mutual. I want to lick you all over, too."

The way he says it, like a dirty promise, makes me groan.

"Oh, Will." I arch beneath him, and add, "Please, please, take off my clothes."

He does as I ask, and soon we are both bare. To my surprise and delight, Will proceeds to do exactly what he stated he wanted to do—he licks me. Not all over, but almost. And, more importantly, his tongue quickly finds the one place that really matters. "God, Will."

"Come for me," he whispers, his voice muffled, by me.

I come for him, hard, against his mouth, and he moves up my body, fast, allowing me little time to recover. Pressing his weight to me, Will kisses me so deeply, so all consuming-like, that I grow crazy with lust.

When he finally gives me a reprieve, I am gasping, and I can't stop circling my hips up against him. "I want more," I whisper.

"How much more?"

"Everything."

He leans over the bed and fishes a condom from his jeans.

As he rises to his knees and rips open the wrapper with his teeth, he asks, "Are you sure?"

I nod, and he swiftly slides the latex down his impressive length.

A few seconds later, Will is back between my legs, pushing inside me.

Oh, wow, this is it.

I wince and pretend the moan I utter is due to pleasure, not pain.

Yeah, I'd rather Will not know this is my first time.

TWENTY-THREE

Will

WHEN I roll off Emma, sated and exhausted, I notice she's extremely quiet.

I lean over to kiss her, but she turns her head.

"Hey, what's wrong?" I ask.

"Nothing," she murmurs.

"Okaaay." I resist the urge to roll my eyes.

She seemed so cool with everything that was happening. Now, she's acting strange. *Whatever*. At the moment, my main concern is ditching the condom on my softening cock.

"Hey, I'm gonna run to the bathroom, okay?"

"Yeah, fine."

When I return from taking care of business, I flip back the covers.

What the...?

Now I know what's up with her. I *see* it, right before my eyes. *Shit*. No wonder she was so freaking tight.

"Christ, Emma. You're a virgin?" I blurt out.

"Yeah," she whispers, and then qualifies, "I mean, I was. But, obviously, not after what we just did."

I close my eyes. God, I feel like the world's biggest prick.

"Emma, if I'd known..." I trail off and sit down on the edge of the bed. Placing my head in my hands, I say, "Christ, you should've told me."

"You wouldn't have done it then, Will."

I lift my head from my hands and stare at her, somewhat shocked by her blasé attitude. Does she really feel that way, or is this just a farce.

"Don't girls usually want their first time to be special?" I ask.

She shrugs and looks away, and I'm still not sure what she's really feeling.

Sighing, I say, "Listen, Emma. The truth is, I wouldn't have had sex with you had I known. Especially not like the way we did it." She groans, like hearing this hurts, and I'm quick to add, "I don't mean I wouldn't have still wanted to be with you. I want you, Emma. I did, and I still do. But we could've waited, taken things more slowly —"

Her head jerks back to me and deep blue eyes flash with anger. "Don't you get it, Will?" She gathers the covers from around her and sits up abruptly. "I was ready. I've waited long enough already. I'm, like, crazy-attracted to you, and it felt right. It was time, and to be honest, I wouldn't change a thing."

"Seriously?" I hope she's telling the truth.

"Yes, Will, seriously." She sounds annoyed, but then she softens when she says, "Besides, it's not like I don't have *any* experience. I've dated guys before you, and I've done all the stuff we did. Just...not that."

I glance at the bloodstain on the sheet, and Emma's quick to cover it with a blanket.

"Did it hurt?" I ask.

She shrugs. "A little. But only really just at first."

I scoot over to her. Wrapping my arms around her, I say, "I still wish you would've told me. I would have gone much easier on you. Like, been gentler, you know."

I would've gone easier on her, too. I certainly wouldn't have pounded into her like I did near the end.

She leans back and peers at me with those bright blue eyes. God, she is so beautiful. And so sexy too, with her hair all sex-tousled.

I brush back a single raven strand, and she lowers the sheet from her chest. "You could show me now," she says.

Trailing my hand down her side, over the swell of her hip, I playfully ask, "Show you what?"

"How you would've gone easier on me."

My cock stirs. I can't deny that I like how I'm the only man who's ever been inside this girl. And I want to be inside her again. In fact, I want her over and over. But this time, this next shot, it's going to be solely for her.

The second time I have Emma Metzger, I do everything for her. I'm careful and gentle, and when, at the end, she calls out my name, I know beyond a shadow of a doubt that she is now all mine.

Only problem is, I'm beginning to feel overwhelmed, maybe even a little bit trapped. And I can't help but ask myself, with all my newfound responsibilities regarding Lily, do I really want something serious with Emma?

TWENTY-FOUR

Emma

WILL doesn't stay the rest of the night. He tells me it's because he knows I have to work the next day, he says I need to get my sleep.

Yeah, right.

I sense his departure is due to something else entirely, like, say, maybe I scared him off with the whole virgin thing. Sure, he mentioned giving dating a try when he first arrived last night. But that was before we had sex. I'm sure he never expected me to be so inexperienced. Hell, he probably thinks because of that that I'm in love with him now. And though I do like Will quite a lot, I don't love him.

He was spooked, though, no doubt about that. After the second time we had sex, he got dressed right away. And yes, he kissed me good-bye and said he'd call, but I'm not holding my breath. Just because I was a virgin until yesterday doesn't mean I'm clueless about men and their shady ways.

Still, though... Do I plan to let Will blow me off without an explanation?

Not a chance.

On Tuesday, when he brings Lily to daycare, I corner him in a hall and ask him if we can go to lunch so we can talk about what happened.

He hems and haws, shifting from one foot to the other.

Finally, he says, "Uh, I don't think today is going to work. I'm supposed to meet Chase in a few. He wants me to take a look around a job site and decide whether or not I want to work for him. You know, building houses and shit."

I know Will needs a job now that he's given up the one in New York, but I can't imagine glancing around a work site is something that takes all day.

With that in mind, I press. "What time are you supposed to meet Chase? We could go to lunch before or after."

Will looks at his watch. "I'm supposed to meet him at ten. And it could take a while."

I resist the urge to roll my eyes at his persistence in pretending this will turn into an all-day event.

"Okay, fine. What about tonight, then?" I counter, abandoning the lunch idea. "I could make us dinner."

"Uh..."

Before he outright declines, I hurriedly add, "You could bring Lily, if you want."

There, that's about as non-date as one can get.

Will reluctantly accepts, and we finalize the details before he leaves.

After work, I race home to start on dinner. I decide to go with something simple: salad and spaghetti. Plus, kids love spaghetti, right? Crap, I sure hope Lily does.

My worry turns out to be for naught, as Will shows up alone. Alone, and looking sexy as hell, in faded jeans and an ecru button-down, I might add.

Gesturing with a bottle of red wine in his hand, he says, "I brought us some wine for tonight, since I'm flying solo."

I smile and accept his gift. "Thanks," I say. And then, stepping back, I beckon for him to follow me to the kitchen.

"So," I toss out over my shoulder, "why didn't Lily want to come along? I made spaghetti, hoping she'd like it."

"Lily loves spaghetti," Will tells me as I stop at the stove and stir the pasta. "But she wanted to stay at the house and play with Sarah." He leans his hip against the side of a counter. "They were deeply involved in a tea party for a bunch of stuffed animals. I couldn't end that, you know?"

I laugh, look over at him. "Well, I guess it's just you and me, then."

"Guess so."

I'm wearing the same clingy purple dress I had on the first day Will ever brought Lily to daycare. I noticed him checking me out that day, and I catch him doing the same thing now. Just as I hoped he would. After all, a girl has to bring her A-game if she expects to win the prize. And, to me, Will is a prize. I want to take a stab at a relationship with him. I think we could be good. He's either going to give this burgeoning relationship a chance—like he said he wanted to—or at least give me a damn good reason why we shouldn't try.

Dinner ends up going smoothly. We eat, drink wine, and talk. I tell Will the wine he brought is outstanding. I don't know if it really is, but it sure does tastes good. And it definitely takes the edge off.

Once the dishes are cleared, I suggest we move to the sofa and have another glass, or two.

"So, Will." I pour a second glass of wine for myself. "How'd your meeting with Chase go today?" I lean back in the crook of the sofa, curling my legs up under me and exposing lots of thigh in the process.

Let's show this boy what he'll be missing if he runs for the hills.

My efforts don't go unnoticed. Will takes a slow sip of wine, glancing at my legs. When he lowers his glass, he licks his lips. I am instantly aroused as I recall all the sinful things Will did with his tongue the other night.

Clearing my throat, and getting a grip, I say, "So, I'm assuming it went well, yes?"

His eyes flicker to my face. "What went well?"

Ah, I have him flustered. Good.

"Your meeting with Chase, of course."

"Oh." Will leans forward and sets his wineglass on the coffee table. "Yes, it went really well."

"So, are you going to take the job?"

Will nods. "Yeah, I think so. But I told Chase I only want a couple of days a week. Nothing more. I still plan on looking for some freelance work."

"Oh, that's right," I say as I suddenly recall Will's one-time dream. "Does that mean you still have plans to have your comic book published?"

Will's brows go up in surprise. "You actually remember me telling you that, all those years ago at the reception?"

I smile at him. "Yeah, actually I do."

Will reaches for his wineglass and takes a small sip. "If I do go that route, I think I'd want to turn my comic book into a graphic novel first. But yeah, bottom line is I still hope to see it in print someday."

"I'd like to see your work." I pause. "If you don't mind, that is."

Will actually blushes, melting me further. I suppose I do like him more than I should. Hell, I know I could fall for him. Completely, if he'd let me.

"Yeah, sure," he says. "I'm flattered you're even

interested in taking a look at the things I've drawn."

"Of course I'm interested, Will."

Our eyes meet and a million unsaid things pass, but then he looks away. "Can I ask you something, Emma?"

"Yes, of course."

Will downs the rest of his wine and sets the glass on the coffee table, this time with a loud clink. "Why were you waiting to have sex?"

I blow out a breath. "I don't know. It wasn't some great moral decision, if that's what you're thinking. I had dozens of chances at college with the various guys I dated. But, I don't know… I guess none of them seemed worth it. I was probably, stupidly, waiting for someone special to come into my life."

"And he never came around?"

Carefully, I reply, "No, not back then."

"Emma," Will says on a sigh. "I have a lot on my plate right now—"

"I know, Will"

"Just hear me out, okay?" I nod, and he goes on. "Not only am I taking care of a daughter I never knew existed, but I'm back to searching for a job in my field. The recruiter who landed me the job in New York City handed me off to another recruiter, one who can hopefully find me a few freelance advertising gigs. Still, it's going to take some time, especially for me to get my name and work out there. That's why I took the job with Chase. I may have a trust fund, but I can't sit around all day and do nothing."

I drink down the last of my wine, hoping to build up some courage. "Look, Will," I say, twirling the stem of the empty wineglass between my fingers. "*You* were the one who came to my door the other night. *You* asked for a second chance. *You* were the one who said you wanted to see where this thing between us might go."

"Yes, I did all those things."

"So, what changed?"

He can't look me in the eyes when he says, "It just felt different, you know…after we had sex."

I scoff in reply, "You mean after you found out it had been my first time."

His eyes flitter over to me for an instant. Then, he's back to staring down at his hands. Quietly, he says, "It suddenly seemed like things were moving way too fast. You know, like maybe you were about to expect a lot from me."

"Will, please." I am sure to make my annoyance known.

Still, he goes on. "Look, I know it makes me sound like a prick, but I just don't have *that* much to give you right now."

He's not entirely wrong in his perception of what I want from him. My feelings for him are intense, and I'd love it if he felt the same way. *Maybe in time?* For now, though, I don't want to scare him off.

Grasping at straws to keep this thing between us alive, I tone down the intensity of my feelings, and say, "I think you read it wrong, Will."

He raises a brow. "I did?"

"Uh-huh. Just because I was looking for Mr. Right in college doesn't mean that's how I feel now. I told you, I was just sick of waiting."

"Oh."

He sounds miffed. *Doesn't feel so good to be used, does it, Will?*

"I just went with the flow the other night," I continue. "You can't deny there's an intense chemistry between us." He nods, agreeing, and I add, "Well, it got the better of us both, and what happened, happened."

Skeptically, Will asks, "That's really how you see it? That cut and dry?"

"Yes," I fib.

He exhales in what I suspect is relief, and my heart suffers the blow. Shit, he's glad. I obviously like Will *way* more than I should. Too bad my feelings for him aren't so easily turned off. And if I sleep with him again, forget it. I *will* end up falling for him completely. *Crap.*

Lucky for me, my heart is spared when Will says, "Still, I think we should slow things down considerably."

I reply, probably a little too quickly, "I couldn't agree more."

Will peers over at me, like he's trying to figure out what's in my head. But he'll never know, not when things are this uncertain between us.

Finally, he says, "We should probably go somewhere where we're not alone."

He's right. The urge to be together again is just too strong.

"Where do you want to go?" I ask.

Standing, he offers me his hand. "How about we go see a movie?"

Before I take his hand, and because I have a shred of dignity left, I raise a brow. "Is this a date?"

"Do you want this to be a date?"

I nod. "I think so."

Chuckling, Will says, "Then, yes, it's a date."

I take his hand.

One date leads to two, and then two to three. And, soon enough, Will and I are officially "dating." We do as agreed, too—we take things slowly. That means no sex, which isn't easy for either of us.

Thank God we can still kiss like crazy, seeing as I love kissing Will Gartner. He's so good at it. He has a way of making me feel like I'm sexy and beautiful and he *needs* to devour me.

We kiss a lot—in Will's car, on my sofa, outside the cinema, on the sidewalks in front of restaurants—everywhere, really. As far as I'm concerned, his lips can't be on me nearly enough.

We also learn to savor the tease and the promise of more. I know when we're together again it will be amazing, especially since we're building a friendship first this time around.

But friendship is far from Will's mind when, during one of our heated make-out sessions, this particular one occurring on my sofa, he groans in my ear, "I can't wait much longer, Emma. I fucking want you so much."

It's not his words alone that make me almost give in. No, it's the wanton need and lust in his tone, and the way he's grinding into me.

I fight to remain strong. *The wait will be worth it*, I remind myself.

Kissing along Will's freshly shaven jaw, I whisper, "Not yet,"—he groans—"but soon."

A flurry of hot kisses is then deposited on one cheek and down my neck.

And finally, against my collarbone, Will whispers what I've longed to hear, "You're making me fall for you, Emma Metzger."

"Good," I whisper back. "Because I've already fallen for you, Will Gartner."

TWENTY–FIVE

Will

I LIKE Emma, I do. We go to movies and restaurants and binge-watch TV shows at her apartment. Most nights, though, we only make it through an episode or two. We grow restless, distracted by each other and the extreme passion between us. Those times, we kiss and grind on the sofa, leaving me to have to take care of things for myself back at the farmhouse. Christ, it's like being a teen again.

But I like this waiting. Being with Emma the next time will be worth it.

Okay, okay, yes, she's also becoming important to me. And because of that we start to do a lot with Lily. My daughter adores Emma, and why wouldn't she? Emma treats Lily like she's her own. It's not an act, either. I really believe Emma loves my little Lil.

Other things are good too.

On the work front, apart from my job with Chase, I land a cool freelance gig. It's just a small job for a regional food chain, but still, it's a start. The company's marketing people want me to come up with a summer advertising campaign, one highlighting how very kid-friendly the chain is.

After a long day at one of Chase's work sites, I stop by the farmhouse, take a quick shower, and, with Lily in tow, head over to Emma's place. The plan is to brainstorm with her about which direction I should take with this advertising project.

An hour later, with storyboards spread across the coffee table in her living room, Emma and I fall into a heated debate on whether to include the chain's famous talking brownie in the campaign.

"The talking brownie is in *all* the campaigns, Will," Emma says, insistent that this is the way to go.

"That's exactly why I think we should mix it up and ditch the brownie," I counter.

"Kids love that brownie, though. And this campaign is supposed to focus on the kid's menu, right?"

"Yeah, yeah, I guess." I run my hand through my hair, at an impasse. "Let's ask Lily what she thinks," I suggest.

Lily is on the floor, coloring some random cartoon character in a coloring book.

"Hey, Lil," I say. "Can I ask you a question?"

Without looking up, she replies in a totally serious voice, "I'm kinda busy."

I snicker. The girl is too much sometimes.

"Well, when you have a minute, Daddy needs your input."

She peers up at me. "What in-put mean?"

I love her endless curiosity. "It's like an opinion."

She taps a crayon to her chin, and I just about lose it. She's seen me do that move a hundred times when I'm working through something. Not with a crayon, but usually with a pen, or a colored pencil, often when I'm drawing with her.

Emma grabs my arm and squeezes. "She's such a mini-you," she whispers, her free hand flying to her mouth to suppress a giggle.

When Lily adds in a contemplative nod, Emma squeezes harder. Now, we're both trying hard as hell not to laugh. *How stinking cute is this kid?*

"Yes," Lily says, at last. "I think I can give you my input, Daddy."

"Thanks, Lil."

I show her the storyboards with the brownie, holding them up against the ones I drew without the silly chocolate character. "Which ones do you like best, sweetheart?" I ask.

More contemplation, more chin tapping, and finally an answer. "I like the brownie."

Emma pumps her fist in victory since she called it. "Yes!"

I roll my eyes. "Women," I mutter.

But truthfully, these are my girls and I wouldn't trade them for the world.

My little girl is well aware she has me wrapped around her finger, so she knows I won't deny her when she asks out of the blue, "Can we go get ice cream?"

"Sure," I reply.

See, I'm a pushover. And, yeah, okay, I spoil my kid. But she deserves it. Lily's a pretty good little girl. She accepts her life here in Harmony Creek, and rarely, if ever, asks about her old life, including her mother.

I sigh as I think about Cassie. Shit. I know if I intend to keep Lily—and I do—I need to reach out to my ex-girlfriend and have her sign full custody over to me. Otherwise, she could come back into our lives and cause trouble. I sure as hell don't need trouble, not when everything has been going so well.

Emma, picking up on my worry, whispers, "Is everything okay?"

I watch as she sits on the floor to help Lily put on her sneakers. Do I see a future with Emma in my life and Lily's?

Yeah, I think I do.

Smiling, I lean down and kiss Emma lightly on the lips. "Everything is awesome, babe."

TWENTY-SIX

Emma

O N a hot July day, Will decides to move into the apartment above the garage at Chase's place. It's not a totally out-of-the-blue decision. He's already checked into other options, including viewing a neighboring apartment at my complex. In the end, though, he's chosen to stay at the farmhouse, for Lily's sake. She loves her cousins dearly, and Will claims he can't bear to separate them a mere month and a half after Lily's mother abandoned her.

"She needs stability," Will tells me at the end of moving day as we discuss his decision.

We're finishing up in his new living room, having just installed a window air conditioner to cool things down.

As I swipe away sweat from my forehead, I say, "I know, Will. You made the right decision." I gesture around the loft. "It's really nice up here."

"It is," he agrees, glancing around himself. "Just a little

on the warm side."

I laugh and make a production of fanning myself. "Yeah, you could say that."

Turning the A/C unit on high, he strolls over to me. "There." Wrapping his arms around me, he says, "It should cool down in here in no time at all."

"Uh, not if you keep pressing up against me like that," I reply, a little on the breathy side…and not from the heat.

Will discarded his T-shirt hours ago, claiming it was too hot. Now, with his bare chest pressed to my cotton tee-clad torso, I am heating up far beyond what the now-cooling room was doing to me a few minutes ago.

I've spent the whole day sneaking peeks at a partially clothed Will. Working for Chase, engaging in lots of physical labor, has left him tanned, tight, and more toned than ever.

I sigh, and he nuzzles his nose against my neck. "Maybe that's my intention," he whispers against my skin.

"Mmm, Will."

I run my hands up his back, his muscles flexing and tensing beneath my touch. He lets out a shiver. "Emma…"

With my lips brushing over his, I tell him, "I think we should move this to the bedroom."

Pulling back, he raises a brow. "You're sure?"

I nod. "Yes. I think it's time."

I'm happy we slowed things down after our frenzied beginning, but I'm ready now to pick up where we left off. Only this time we'll be building our physical relationship on a strong foundation, one comprised of friendship and genuine caring.

Though the living room was cooling rapidly, I find it's warm and muggy in the bedroom. I like it, however. I want nothing more than to have Will's hot, sweaty skin pressed to mine. It makes this need feel more urgent.

And urgent is what we are. We kiss and grope and

shed our clothes in no time.

And then we're lying on the bed.

"You taste salty," I whisper as I lick and kiss along Will's chest and abs.

"Just, whatever you do, don't stop what you're doing right the hell now," he rasps. "Please."

I know the feeling. Now that we're starting back down this road, I couldn't stop if I wanted to.

Moving farther and farther down Will's body, I find him hard and ready. When I take his swollen cock in my mouth, he arches and groans. It's not just salt I taste now, it's the essence of what makes Will male.

While I do sinful things to this man with my mouth and my tongue, he shifts my body till my sex is positioned above his head. And then he lifts up and flicks his tongue over my clit, leaving me mumbling from around his shaft, "OhmyGodWillyes."

Grasping my hips and shoving me down onto his face, he licks and laps until I come, over and over.

Before I have a chance to recover, I am tossed onto my back. "Mmm, Will," I purr.

I like this aggressive, commanding version of him, especially when he rises to his knees and nudges my legs wide, wide, wider. When I am fully exposed to him, I let my body go lax. I want to convey to Will that I am his to do with whatever he chooses. My body belongs to him in this moment—to take pleasure from, to toy with, whatever he desires.

His eyes scan up my body, and I know he's contemplating what to do with me next. *Good.*

What he ultimately chooses to do is grab hold of his thick shaft, his large hand cresting over the crown. "Do you want this?" he asks.

"Yes," I whisper.

"Louder," he says as he presses the head of his cock to

my wet folds.

"Yes," I say louder.

He pulls back, but only for a sec. Just long enough to slide a condom down his length. And then he's right back on me, at my entrance, pressing, pressing, my legs pushed back even farther.

"I don't think I heard you, Emma," he says.

"Yes, Will, yes!" His cock pierces me then, and I take him... I just take all of him inside my body.

Our movements are fierce at first—primal, even—but then Will slows things down. He lowers my raised legs and settles his body between my thighs. Slowly and methodically, with a measured in and out rhythm, Will Gartner fucks me.

Wrapping his hands in my hair and burying his face in the crook of my neck, he pushes in as far as he can go. "Emma." He circles his hips. "I need you so much."

I catch my breath. Will has never shown this level of vulnerability before today. I swallow the lump that forms in my throat and hold onto him more tightly. God, I need him, too. But that's not what comes out of my mouth. It's some garbled declaration of devotion, one that may or may not contain the word "love."

He lifts his head, so he can see my face, though he remains deep inside of me. "What did you say?" he asks.

There's no hiding, no running away. Not only is Will buried deep in my body, he's lodged securely in my heart.

I may as well tell him, I decide.

"I love you," I say.

I don't know what I expect—maybe him pulling out, dressing, and running off?

That doesn't happen. Thank God.

What Will does is still my hips so I can feel him filling me so completely. He then leans down till our foreheads touch.

And then, just as he starts to move, he says, "I love you, too."

After a second round of sex, this one accompanied by more whispered words of love, Will and I wrap up in each other's arms and talk late into the night. I bring him up to speed on all the über-excitement down at the school. And though Will snoozes through most of my little-kid daycare stories, he perks up and listens to each and every tale that pertains to Lily.

When I'm done, we switch over to his work life, and he tells me of another freelance job coming his way.

"That's great." I cup the side of his face and plant a kiss on his scruffy jaw.

"Thanks, babe," he says when I lean back. "I still wish more was happening on the freelance front."

Will loves making magic with his art. When he's drawing, the passion he feels is so evident. It's especially adorable when he draws with Lily. She tries so hard to replicate her father's style, but she's too young to get it down exactly. Still, like what we witnessed at the school, her technique is solid. She's pretty darn good at drawing cartoon-style animals, that's for sure.

Thinking of cartoons reminds me of Will's comic book and his graphic novel plans, leading me to inquire, "Can I ask you something, Will?"

He shimmies closer to me. "Sure."

"How are things going with that graphic novel plan?"

He makes a face. "Uh, I'd say it's not going at all, since I've done nothing with it."

"Will."

"Emma."

I prop up on an elbow. "What are you waiting for? I thought you wanted to turn your comic book into a graphic novel and have the thing published?"

"Eh." He shrugs, making the sheet edge down to expose his hard, flat abs. "I haven't had the time to do anything with it, not with working for Chase and taking care of Lily. Although…"

"Yeah?"

"I printed out a list of agents who'd rep me for something like that."

Excitedly, I say, "That's awesome. You should submit your work, like, to all of them, and see what happens."

"I guess so, Emma." Will makes a sweeping motion to all the boxes we didn't get around to unpacking. "The list is somewhere in one of those cartons. I'll get to it, eventually."

Hmmm, I wonder.

I can tell from Will's resigned affect that his dream has taken a backseat to everything else in his life. But it needn't be that way. Like with any man, Will simply needs a good woman to get the ball rolling.

And I am that woman.

If I plan to keep my intentions from Will, however, I conclude it's probably best to end the conversation for now.

Yawning, I murmur, "Wow, I'm exhausted. We should probably get some sleep, yeah?"

"Probably," Will agrees, yawning, as well.

Ten minutes later, after Will has fallen asleep, I slip out from under the covers. It takes me a good half an hour to find the printout of the agents, but when I do, I tuck that damn list in my purse.

There, done.

Now I just have to bide my time till I can move onto step number two—copying the file of Will's comic book from his computer to a flash drive. Shouldn't be too hard, I just need access to his laptop.

Will doesn't know it yet, but once I have that file in my hands, I plan to query every agent on the list I just nabbed. I want nothing more than to help Will make his dreams come true, especially since I love him.

And also because, though I kind of find it hard to believe, Will Gartner loves me.

TWENTY-SEVEN

Will

'VE fallen for Emma Metzger. That's why I told her I love her, because, damn it, I do. Thank God she loves me, too.

The week after I move into the apartment above the garage—and following my and Emma's declarations of love—Chase and I begin a new routine of kicking back in his living room after work. Some days we drink a beer or two, but most days we're content with just pop.

Like today. I'm chilling on the sofa, downing an icy-cold Cherry Coke, while Chase is reclined in an easy chair across from me. He's drinking the same generic lemon-lime pop he's loved for years.

"Dude," I say, chuckling, "I can't believe you still like that stuff."

"Like it, little bro?" He raises his can in salute. "I love this shit. And besides, when you find a good thing, you should stick with it."

"Isn't that the truth," I mumble as I lean forward and

set my Cherry Coke can on the coffee table between us.

When I glance up, Chase is eyeing me curiously.

Settling back on the sofa cushions, I say, "I know that look, Chase. What is it you're dying to ask me?"

He laughs. "Okay, yeah. There *is* something I've been meaning to ask."

"Go ahead, shoot."

He finishes off his beloved lemon-lime and sets the can on the floor by his chair. "Just wondering how things are going with you and Emma," he says.

Chase has stayed out of my business for the most part, but since he's partnered with Emma's cousin's husband, I knew this would eventually come up.

"Don't worry," I begin in my most reassuring voice. "Emma is cool. I have no plans to do her wrong and cause a war between you and your business partner."

Chase arches a brow. "So, what are you saying? Are things getting serious with you two?"

A rush of panic hits me. "Whoa, slow down, bro. We just went exclusive."

Chase shakes his head, like I have no clue. "Just watch it, Will. Girls like Emma tend to get real serious real quick."

"We did say the words," I admit.

"What? The dreaded 'I love yous'?"

I blow out a breath. "Those would be the ones."

I love Emma, but sharing it with my brother makes it feel so fucking real. Not to mention, scary as fucking hell. Maybe because the only other time I loved a girl was throughout my misspent youth with Cassie. And we all know how that turned out.

As if to punctuate my growing list of responsibilities that have me panicked, Lily begins giggling and screeching something incoherent, her voice shrill from out in the backyard where the kids are playing.

After a quick glance to an open window facing where

the kids are, Chase says, "Hey, look, I'm happy things are going so well for you and Emma. Truly, dude, I am—"

"Thanks, man."

"—but I have to ask," Chase drones right over me. "You two are being safe, right?"

I roll my eyes. "You're seriously asking me that question?"

"Yeah, I am, Will. I love your daughter, don't get me wrong, but one little Lil is enough…for now."

"You don't have to worry," I assure Big Bro. "Emma started taking the pill a while back, and I'm still using condoms in the interim."

Chase releases a pent-up breath. "Well, that's a relief to hear."

Our conversation is mercifully interrupted then when our rambunctious children move playtime from the backyard to the living room.

"Hey, no running in the house," Chase calls out to Jack when he scampers into the room, the girls trailing behind him.

Jack skids to a stop, and Sarah and Lily just about collide into his back. Chase and I can't help but laugh at their antics. Some days, I swear, it's like a comedy show around this house.

"Come over here," Chase says to his kids.

Sarah and Jack make a beeline for their dad and clamber up into his lap. Lily plops down on the floor by my feet, and I reach down and ruffle her hair.

Batting my hand away, she chirps, "Daddy, my hair! You're messing it all up."

"You're such a girl," I tease.

Hands on her hips, she twists around and glares up at me. "I *am* a girl," she feels fit to inform me. Like this is something I haven't quite figured out.

Chuckling, I say, "Yes, I know, sweetheart."

"I'm a girl like Miss Emma."

"Yes, Emma is a girl, too."

She points over to Sarah, who's watching our exchange with rapt attention from Chase's lap. Jack has already gotten down and is taking the batteries out of the remote control for the TV, for no apparent reason. He's just inquisitive like that.

"Sarah's a girl, too," Lily states, her tone serious.

"Yep, she is."

"I am," Sarah reaffirms, in a tiny voice that makes Chase smile. He leans down and kisses the top of her head.

Meanwhile, out of the clear blue, Jack points the remote to his crotch and announces, "And I'm a boy!"

Chase and I burst out laughing once more.

"He just discovered not everyone has a penis," Chase informs me in a soft voice.

"Aha."

As I'm nodding in understanding, Lily, clearly having heard Chase, wants to know, "What's a pe-nith?"

"Uh..."

I look to Chase for guidance, but since Sarah isn't one bit interested in the answer to Lily's question, I know he's not going to get involved.

"Sorry, bro," he says, confirming my suspicions. "You're on your own for this one."

"Thanks," I deadpan.

I have no clue where to start this explanation, and it shows. "Uh, well, Lily. It's hard to explain—"

Jack suddenly interrupts with, "I can show you."

As his hands go to the sides of his elasticized waist shorts, Chase and I both yell, "No!"

Thankfully, Jack listens.

He shrugs, like he has no idea what the big deal is, and soon his attention returns to messing with the remote.

Lily, still intent on finding out what a penis is, says,

"I'll ask Miss Emma."

I have no qualms about passing this off to someone else. I know Lily will never remember, anyway. "Good plan," I say. "Definitely ask Miss Emma. She knows. Daddy makes sure of that all the time."

Chase, shaking his head, murmurs, "That's just wrong, bro."

Resting her head against my calf, Lily inquires, "Is Miss Emma going to be my new mommy?"

"Whoa, where's this coming from?" I want to know.

Lily doesn't answer my question, she simply says, "I like Miss Emma, Daddy. She's nice."

"She *is* nice, Lil. I like her, too."

This conversation, though not ideal, is easier to deal with than the penis one. Or so I think.

When Lily then informs me, "I tell all the kids at daycare that Miss Emma gonna be my mom," I am suddenly not so sure.

I look over at Chase, and he lets out a long sigh. "Hey, guys," he says to Jack and Sarah. "Let's go outside so Uncle Will can talk with Lily."

His kids are up for going back outside to play, especially since their dad is joining them this time around.

The room is emptied in seconds, and once I'm alone with Lily I tell her not to tell people, kids or adults, things like that.

"Why?" she asks.

"Because we don't know what's going to happen in the future, Lil."

"So, Miss Emma will never be my mommy, like, ever, ever?"

Lord, give me strength.

I tell her the truth. "I don't know, Lily."

She peers up at me, sadness clear in her emerald eyes as she asks, "Is Emma going to leave us?"

"Oh, Lil...." I lift her up to my lap and hold onto her tightly. "No, sweetheart, I think Emma's the sticking-around type."

"You promise she won't leave like Mommy did?"

"No, Lily. Emma would never do something like that. She's not anything like your mommy."

And she's not. Cassie and Emma couldn't be any more different than the sun and the moon. And who they are — or were — in my life is vastly different, too. Cassie represents my past, a time filled with drugs, anger, and recklessness. If not for Lily, I'd choose to erase it all.

Emma, conversely, represents my future. Or she could, if I let her. A future with Emma would be a good one too, days filled with love, comfort, and support.

Who wouldn't want that, right?

TWENTY-EIGHT

Emma

F OR a solid week, I'm too busy with work, and spending time with Will, to find time to copy the e-file of his comic book file so I can secretly send out query letters for him. That doesn't mean I don't grab the opportunity to do exactly that when Will runs out one weekend night to pick up a pizza for us.

It's Friday, our official movie-and-dinner evening. This "date" is being spent at Will's place, since Lily wanted to sleep over at the farmhouse with her cousins. We're thrilled to have a chance to be alone all night. But, for the moment, Will leaving to pick up the pizza has fortuitously left me all alone in his apartment.

Time to go a-searching…

I feel bad for snooping through the files on Will's laptop — which he conveniently left out on the coffee table in the living room — but I continuously remind myself that this breach of trust is for a good reason. I don't really pay attention to what he has on his computer anyway, as I'm primarily focused on finding the comic book file.

But then I come upon his spank bank of porn, and, well, I just have to take a minute to peruse.

"Hmm, interesting," I murmur after a few minutes of checking things out.

Will's porn collection *is* interesting. It's comprised mostly of video clips—hot, little snippets of all kinds of action. The content is so raw and real that my own juices soon get flowing. There's one of a pizza delivery guy delivering far more than pizza that I just have to watch all the way through.

When I start squirming around on the sofa, wishing fervently that Will was back, I make myself close the clip.

"Wow, Will." I fan myself, trying to cool down. "I sure wish we could re-enact that one."

Too bad I can't share my desire with Will, as I bet he'd be up for it, in more ways than one.

Focus, Emma!

A few minutes pass—and with my libido at bay, for the time being—I soon stumble upon the draft of Will's comic book. Opening the file, I start a slide show of cells Will originally drew with his own hand.

"Amazing," I whisper as the colorful scenes quickly flow into a gripping story.

I shake my head, impressed. Will is so damn unbelievably talented.

From what I can gather—since I don't have time to check out the whole book—his story revolves around a lead character named Champion, a muscle-bound guy who looks remarkably similar to Chase.

I have to smile. Will loves his brother so very much.

In Champion's world, dark days have arrived. Crime runs rampant in a war-devastated Las Vegas. The subject matter is dark, yet somehow filled with hope. Champion is a kind of vigilante, one who imparts his own brand of justice. He helps the poor and downtrodden, and eventually they rise up against a criminal ring running Sin City.

Quickly, I reach down to the floor and rummage through my purse to find the flash drive I brought. Once I have the drive in hand, I shove it into the USB port and swiftly copy the file.

Just in time, too.

After placing the flash drive back in my bag, Will strolls in with the pizza.

I slam the lid down on his laptop and thrust myself back on the sofa cushions.

Not noticing that anything is up, Will holds the pizza box aloft, and says, "Hope you're hungry, babe. This thing is huge. The large-size pie here is way bigger than the pizza I'm used to getting out west."

"As long as you remembered pepperoni, I'm sure I can manage to eat my fair share," I say, hoping I don't look as guilty as I feel.

"Yep, I remembered," Will tells me. "I even asked for extra."

It's then I notice that although I closed the laptop, I forgot to power it down. The on-light is glowing bright green, like an accusatory eye.

Crap. I better distract Will so he doesn't notice.

"You're the best boyfriend ever," I suddenly start gushing as I flip my hair over my shoulder in what I hope is a sexy manner. "Maybe we should skip the pizza and go right to your reward."

Will looks utterly confused. "Reward?"

Think fast.

"Yes," I purr, batting my lashes. "You deserve a reward for being so thoughtful and remembering that I love pepperoni."

Placing the pizza box on the island that separates the kitchen from the living room, Will eyes me curiously. "Are you feeling all right, Emma?" he asks.

I sigh.

And then I come clean.

Well, kind of.

Since I can't tell Will what I was really up to—in case none of the agents ever get back to me—I go with a different tact.

"Okay, you found me out." I raise my hands, like *I'm-so-busted*. "Your laptop was sitting here"—I make a dramatic gesture to the laptop—"and I wanted to look up something on Google."

"All right," Will says slowly. "So, what's so awful about that?"

"Um, well, nothing." *Just spit it out.* "It's just that I kind of stumbled upon your porn stash."

Will suppresses a laugh. "I don't care, Emma. You really think I'd be mad about that?"

"Well, yeah, kind of."

He cocks his head, observing me as he asks in a low voice, "Why? What'd you think? Were you offended?"

"Uh... Not exactly." My face warms. No, wait, *everything* warms. "Actually, I thought some of the clips were pretty hot."

Forgetting all about the pizza, Will stalks toward me. "Oh, yeah? Which ones?"

I press back into the cushions, my pulse quickening. "Well, there was one in particular..."

"Go on."

"It's the video where the delivery boy gives the girl, uh, more than the pizza. Anyway, I thought that one was super-hot."

Will, having reached the sofa, stands over me, tall and foreboding. "How fitting then that I just brought in a pizza," he rasps.

"I think so, too." I'm trying to play it shy, like the girl in the video.

Will likes this game, I can tell. His smoldering emerald gaze grows dark. I like the play-acting, too. More than I ever thought I would. I want Will so much that I'm now pulsing in delicious anticipation. We both know the delivery boy took the girl fast and hard, from behind. But first, he made her strip in front of him, while he stood towering over her, barking out lewd commands.

When Will unzips his jeans and demands, "Take your shorts off, slut!" I can't wait to comply.

Wow, am I ever glad I left the laptop on.

TWENTY-NINE

Will

THIS isn't our usual sex, but damn, I definitely like it. I never thought I'd get off so much on commanding Emma to strip out of her clothes — while saying filthy things to her — but fuck, man, I do. It makes me hard as steel, in fact, as I watch her strip to nothing, while I remain clothed, with only my cock out and in my hand.

I stroke myself slowly and watch her perky breasts swing as I command her to, "Get down on your fucking knees. Yeah, like that. Now, show me your hot little pussy."

She complies, and I reach forward with my free hand to pinch one of her nipples. Not hard, just enough to make her squirm. I then do the same as the dude in the video clip and tell Emma, "Get that ass in the air, bitch. Yeah, like that. You're such a dirty girl."

As I deliver a smack to her high-in-the-air ass, Emma lets out a yelp.

"Is it too much?" I ask, slipping out of character long

enough to make sure I don't go too far.

But she assures me, "No, no, keep going. I love this, Will."

Damn, she's not kidding. When I spread her cheeks, her pink folds are glistening, evidence of her excitement.

"You like this, don't you?" I ask as I dip a finger deep in her moisture, making her gasp.

"Yes," she moans as she rocks back and forth on me.

I add a second digit. "Work yourself on my fingers. I want you ready for my cock."

More words from the clip that make Emma even wetter.

"Damn, girl." Those words are my own.

When I remove my fingers, she cries out at the loss. But I'm not done. Squaring up her hips, I press the tip of my dick to her entrance. I give her no more, no less. I then make her beg for it, and she quickly parrots the desperate pleas of the girl in the clip. Only Emma sounds far more convincing than the actress. This is no act for my girl — she really wants me. And, fuck, I want her. But this time I also want to "feel" her, without the fucking condom. She's been on the pill for over thirty days, we should be good.

"Fuck it." I thrust into her, and she pushes back against me, driving me in deeper. "Christ."

"Yes, yes, yes," she chants.

"Is this okay?" I ask, stilling my hips for a sec. "We're good, right?"

"Uh-huh," she breathes out.

"Good."

I proceed to then fuck Emma on the sofa, and on the floor, doggy-style. But then I want more than the video clip reenactment. I want us face-to-face when I make her come, so I can kiss her, seeing as I fucking love this girl.

Draping myself over her back, I lean down and whisper in her ear, "You okay with deviating from the script."

"Yeah," she murmurs.

Pulling out, I turn her around to face me. "This is better, yeah?"

She smiles and agrees, "It is, Will."

Emma stretches out before me on the sofa, and fuck, she looks hot. She beckons me with a curled finger, like I need an invitation.

As I lower my body onto hers, she wiggles beneath me. "Give me all of your weight when you're back inside me," she says, breathing hard. "I love when you do that."

Sheathing myself in her soft canal, I let out a moan. And then, pressing down on her like she asked me to do, I touch my lips to hers. "I love you so much," I whisper.

"I love you, too, Will."

We move as one till she comes apart. And then I follow.

Later, after we're cleaned up and dressed once more, we finally get around to eating the pizza. It's cold, but neither of us cares. We're too famished from our intense activity.

I turn on the TV at some point and we decide on a Netflix movie. It's something old and kind of low-budget-y, but it doesn't matter to me. I'm just happy hanging out with Emma.

But I worry, as well. This isn't my life. My life is fast-paced, punctuated by turmoil.

Still, I could get used to this.

If only my life could remain this carefree and simple.

THIRTY

Emma

SEND out twenty-seven query letters, and then I send out twelve more, all with a sample of Will's work. As my task proceeds, I check off each name on Will's list of agents, the ones supposedly interested in repping an artist like him.

And then I wait.

A week passes...and nothing.

And then it's two weeks without a bite.

Oh, well.

Still, it saddens me that not one of the agents recognizes Will's talent.

Life, meanwhile, as it does, rolls on...

August arrives, and Will enrolls Lily in kindergarten. We go down to the school together to complete the task, and afterward we walk around to the back of the building.

"I want to show you something," I tell Will.

"What? Your flowers?" He gestures to the flower

beds where he found me planting impatiens almost three months ago. "They sure have grown," he murmurs.

"They have," I agree, and then I add, "But, no, silly boy, that's not what I want to show you."

I nudge him in the side with an elbow and he lets out an exaggerated, "Oomph."

Grabbing his hand, I lead him over to a trail that snakes down the side of a wooded terrace. "What I want to show you is down that path."

Following behind me as I step onto the trail, he says, "Ooh, leading me into the deep, dark woods. What exactly do you plan to do with me, naughty girl?"

I let go of his hand so I can turn around and swat his chest. "Nothing like what you're thinking, perv."

"Too bad."

He sounds genuinely disappointed, and I consider for a minute whether we could mess around down in the woods. But then I remember Father Maridale, still up at the school, processing registrations, and I determine messing around is probably not such a good idea.

I duck under a tree branch, and Will reaches forward to lift it out of my way. "Thanks," I say.

"For you, my darling, anything."

I shake my head at his playful and exaggerated tone. "Come on, Mr. Chivalry, we're almost there."

Thirty seconds later, we walk into a clearing. There's an old metal swing set that's no longer in use located smack-dab in the middle of the field.

"This," I say, heading toward the swings with Will trailing behind, "is what I want to show you."

"Pretty cool," he states when we reach the dilapidated, old swing set. "So, how long has this ancient relic been here?"

I smack his arm. "I'd say long before our time, smartass."

When I plop down on the worn wooden seat of one of the swings, Will's brow creases and he asks, "Is that thing safe?"

There are three swings in total, but the wooden seat to the far left rotted in the middle and has since broken in half. Motioning to the busted swing, I reply, "As long as you don't try to sit your ass on that one, you should be fine."

Chuckling, Will plops down on the intact swing next to me. "So, now what happens?" he asks.

I push off. "We swing, silly."

At first, Will is hesitant. He drags his feet back and forth on the ground, his swing barely moving. But once I get going, he soon joins me.

Flying high, to and fro, feels as freeing as it did back when I was a kid. And when Will starts to laugh, I know this is good for him, too. Sometimes you need to let go a little so you can forget the trials of adulthood, even if only for a short while.

When we finally slow our swings, and eventually come to a full stop, we end up talking about Lily and the upcoming school year.

Our childhood foray is over, back to the real world.

Will asks me something about Lily's curriculum, and I remind him that, unlike with daycare, Lily won't be in my class.

"I teach first graders, Will. Remember? It's the same position Kay once held."

Will then proceeds to pepper me with dozens of questions about the current teacher, Mrs. Salazar, a young woman who's due to have a baby in December.

"Is she as good as you?" he asks.

I blush at the compliment. "Yes, Will. She's great. The kids love her."

"But she's taking maternity leave around Christmas,

right? Who'll fill in?"

"I'm not sure," I reply honestly.

"Can I meet this Mrs. Salazar before Lily starts school?"

"I'm sure you can."

"What if Lily doesn't like her?"

I sigh. "Will, really?"

For a guy who once planned to place Lily in twelve hours minimum of daily daycare up in New York City, he sure has changed his tune. Talk about an overly concerned father.

"Everything will be fine," I assure him.

Truthfully, Will's concern for Lily makes me love him even more.

A few days later, and still a couple of weeks before school starts, we get word that Mrs. Salazar has been put on bed rest for the duration of her pregnancy.

"Now what will Lily do?" Will wants to know.

A new wave of worry now plagues the poor guy.

"Father Maridale will find someone competent to take over," I assure him.

"Yeah, like who?"

This conversation occurs in Chase and Kay's dining room. We were invited over for an end-of-summer cookout. Chase is in the back, grilling and watching the kids as they play, and Kay is in the kitchen, which is directly off the dining room. She's boiling freshly picked corn, as I hear her stirring the water.

Kay must hear our discussion of the school situation, for she comes in after a minute, wiping her hands on a dish towel. "Hey, what about me?" she asks, smiling surreptitiously.

I give Will a look that implores: *Do you have any idea what she's talking about?*

He shrugs as Kay walks over to stand next to his chair. Glancing up at her, he asks, "What's up, my favorite sister-in-law?"

She swats him with the towel. "I'm your *only* sister-in-law," she says, rolling her eyes.

"Still my fave," Will states matter-of-factly.

I chuckle at their banter. Will's really becoming an integral part of their family. It's like he was an outsider for so long, mostly of his own doing, but not anymore. He's found his place here.

Will then asks Kay, "So, why do you look so smug?"

"Maybe it's because I have some good news," Kay replies.

"Oh, is it something to do with the school situation?" I interject.

"Yes."

Will puts it together, same as I do, and, as he does, hope blooms in his verdant eyes. "And this good news would be...?" he asks.

Kay is beaming when she announces, "*I* am taking over Mrs. Salazar's kindergarten class."

"That is so awesome," I say.

Will echoes my sentiment, and adds, "Hell, this may be the best news I've heard all day."

Kay goes on to explain how she and Chase mulled it over and ultimately decided that since Jack is starting first grade—in my class—and Sarah will be entering kindergarten with Lily, she may as well go back to work. And the teaching job will keep her close to her kids all day.

"I was originally thinking of picking up a part-time job in town," she informs us. "Like, maybe something at a store or a restaurant. But then Father Maridale called and told me Mrs. Salazar was taking medical leave. He asked if there was any way he could convince me to come back and take over the kindergarten class." She smiles. "Let's just say it didn't take too much convincing."

"This is so great," I reiterate. "Not only will you be

around Sarah and Lily all day, but you'll only be a couple of classrooms away from Jack."

"It is rather perfect," Kay agrees.

Will, of course, remains elated. Chase comes in right then with a platter of burgers and hot dogs. The kids trail behind him, quietly, till they take their seats at the table. Then, it's chatter time.

Over their lively little voices, Chase peers over at Will. "You're smiling, bro, so I take it Kay told you the good news that she's returning to teaching?"

"She sure did," Will replies. "And I couldn't be happier."

Chase laughs. "I bet."

After an amazing dinner, and the rest of the evening spent out in the backyard, I inform everyone that I need to head back to my place. Will asks why, and I fib and say I have some lesson plans to attend to. Really, I'm just anxious to check and see if today brought any responses to the many query letters I'm still waiting to hear back from.

After I arrive home and settle in on the sofa with my laptop, I am pleasantly surprised to discover a reply.

Finally!

It's only one email, but it's more than enough, seeing as it's a positive response. Apparently, the agent who replied to my query letter would *love* to take a look at Will's full comic book manuscript.

Holy crap!

I jump up and do a little dance around my apartment. Yes, I'm overjoyed.

I then print out the letter. Wow, I can't wait to show it to Will.

THIRTY-ONE

Will

FOLLOWING Emma's departure on Friday night, to supposedly work on lesson plans for the upcoming school year, I bid Chase and Kay a good-night, and head over to my apartment above the garage with Lily.

"Are you excited about starting school in a couple of weeks?" I ask my daughter as we walk across the gravel driveway, the late-summer locusts providing a lively chorus in the background.

Lily is skipping, but she slows and takes my hand. "I am ec-cited, Daddy. Did you know Auntie Kay's going to be my teacher?" She smiles up at me, and I find myself smiling right back at her.

"Yeah, Lil, Auntie Kay told me the good news right before dinner."

"I can't wait for school," Lily says softly, her proclamation punctuated with a wide yawn.

My daughter is clearly sleepy from playing for hours

with her cousins.

When she leans up against my leg as we walk, I ask her, "You want me to carry you, princess?"

"Uh-huh."

By the time we're up the wooden stairs and in the apartment, Lily is out. I lay her down gently on her bed.

I finally partitioned the living room to create a proper bedroom for Lily. It isn't huge, but she loves having her own space. The walls in the entire apartment are a neutral off-white color, including Lily's new room, but Emma and I made the area more girly by adding dolls and stuffed animals, along with touches of Lily's favorite colors, lavender and pink. Most of the throw pillows and bedding are those shades.

I smile as I recall how it took me forever to find the comforter Lily saw online when I was showing her stuff we could buy for her room. Only problem was the site we were perusing listed the item as out-of-stock. Lily was so disappointed that I made it my personal mission to find the damn thing, no matter how long it took.

I succeeded, too, and in only a few days' time. After tracking the comforter down at an outlet ninety miles away, I drove out to the store and scooped it up, along with all the matching bedding. Wow, was Lily ever thrilled.

And it's that exact comforter, a frilly lavender affair with "Princess" spelled out in deep purple in the center, that I now gently pull up to Lily's chin.

"Sweet dreams, little Lil," I say as I press a kiss to her forehead.

Over on the side of the room that's still a living room, I plop down on the sofa and turn on my laptop.

"Huh."

There's an email from my old recruiter, marked as urgent. I open it and discover he "needs" to speak with me "as soon as possible."

I take out my cell, find his number in my contacts, and hit *Call*.

Answering on the second ring, the recruiter says excitedly, "Will. Glad you're getting back to me so quickly. I take it you received my email?"

"Yeah, I did. So, what's up?"

"Well, I may have an opportunity for you. It's not with the same company as before, but rather a competitor of theirs. You'd still need to go to New York City. But let me say ahead of time, Will, that these people *want* you. Like, to the point they're willing to go way up on the salary."

"How far up?" I ask, intrigued.

"Twenty-five percent higher than what the other company was willing to pay."

"Wow." I do some quick math calculations in my head. "That kind of money is unheard of for someone fresh out of school."

"What can I say?" he states. "They really, *really* want you."

But I have a life here, my gut urges me to tell this guy. And so does Lily. Wasn't she just telling me how excited she is for school to start?

"Shit."

Sensing my reticence, the recruiter says, "Listen, man, I know you've been landing some freelance advertising work—and that's great and all—but you're never going to make bank and get your name out there in any meaningful way unless you get in with one of these top firms. And, Will, my man, this is a golden opportunity with a top firm."

Don't I know it?

I don't feel elated, like I probably should. Within the course of this five-minute call, I feel more like I've been thrust back to square one, with nothing certain in my life. I feel just like I did the day I arrived in Harmony Creek.

A dozen things run through my mind...

What about Lily starting school?

What about Emma?

What about my new life here with my brother and his wife and kids?

And, in the back of my mind, since I know I haven't given my graphic novel a chance to come to fruition, I think, *What about my dream?*

Sighing, I ask the recruiter, "When would I need to decide?"

I can't believe you're even considering this, an inner voice chastises.

"It's pretty much yours if you want it, but you need to meet the head of advertising before anything is deemed official. The guy you'll need to see is flying up to Chicago this weekend, for some big conference that begins on Monday. So, if you're really interested, Will, you need to drive up on Sunday and meet this guy by nightfall."

"So," I say, calculating drive times, "I basically have until early Sunday morning to decide."

The recruiter sighs. "Look, I'll tell him you're coming, but, yeah, you could always back out by then. If you do, just know it's the end of the line for any more chances like this one. Word will get out and that'll be the end of any more sweet offers."

"Okay, man, I got it."

From there, it's like some unseen clock begins ticking. And, shit, I feel like my time here in Harmony Creek is running out.

THIRTY-TWO

Emma

WILL'S in a shitty mood on Saturday. We're supposed to go out on a breakfast date, but he just called and is canceling on me. He claims he's not feeling well.

Yeah, right. I know he's hiding something.

When he tries to get off the phone, I blurt out, "What's really going on here, Will?"

"Nothing," he says.

"Hey, it's me you're talking to. You can share stuff with me. You know this, right?"

He sighs, and I imagine him dragging his hand through his hair. "I know, Emma." His voice is soft, almost forlorn, and I know for sure something's up.

But before I can press, Lily starts crying in the background, prompting Will to say in a rush, "I have to go."

And then he's gone.

I toss the phone aside and stare down at the letter I printed out, the emailed response from the agent who can't wait to see Will's work. I planned on showing it to him this morning at breakfast.

Alas…

Still, the agent needs an answer, and soon. Offers like these don't hang around indefinitely.

I close my eyes and fall back on my bed. *What should I do?*

If I wait for Will it may be too late. Not to mention, he sure can be a moody bastard at times, like this morning. What if he's feeling pissy and decides he doesn't want to send the agent his work?

I cannot let that happen.

Jumping up, I grab my laptop from the dresser and scramble to find the agent's email.

There.

I type in a professional-sounding reply, one that hopefully seems like it's really from Will and I'm just acting as his representative. Like a publicist, or something. I then attach his complete comic book file.

Squeezing my eyes shut, I hit *Send.*

I sure hope Will doesn't hate me for doing this.

THIRTY-THREE

Will

First thing I do when I wake up on Saturday morning, which is unusually chilly for August, is tug on a pair of sweatpants and grab a long-sleeve T-shirt. Second thing I do, as I'm pulling the tee over my head, is head to Lily's room to talk with her about our potential move.

"Hey, sweetheart." I sit down on the edge of her bed as she opens her eyes, noting how they're as bright and green as her cute pajama set.

Lily sits up and rubs those cute green eyes. "Daddy, what's wrong?"

Crap. Guess I can't hide my apprehension from my child. I just know that my daughter is *not* going to be pumped for another potential move to New York City. She loves it here in Harmony Creek. She has her aunt and uncle and her cousins, whom she adores. Plus, kindergarten is starting soon.

And then there's Emma, whom I know Lily loves

dearly.

Shit. Emma. I'm supposed to meet her for breakfast today. Fuck. I need to cancel that shit. I can't think clearly when I'm around her. My feelings for her cloud my judgment. But since I do love Emma, maybe I could talk her into moving to New York…eventually.

For now, I just need to focus on what's best for me and Lil.

Truthfully, there aren't enough freelance gigs coming in to make creating advertising campaigns my career. And my work with Chase will surely slow by winter. I could always fall back on my trust fund, but, like I've always maintained, I really want to make it on my own. My ultimate goal has always been to show all the doubters that I'm no longer a fuck-up.

There's always the comic book and the graphic novel idea.

Yeah, right. Like anyone would even be interested. It's high time I shelve that old dream.

Lily tugs at the arm of my long-sleeved tee. "Daddy, are you listening?"

She's been chattering, and I *have* missed most of what she's been saying, but I pretend I've heard every peep. "Yes, sweetie, I'm listening."

Her little face scrunches up in a scowl. She knows I'm full of it, plus she suspects something is wrong.

Crossing her arms defiantly, she says, "I want to know why you wake me up."

Sighing, I say, "I need to ask you something, okay? It's something about our future."

Apprehension clouds her face. She knows this drill.

Lily has been bounced around enough times that I'm not the tiniest bit surprised when she says in a tiny, defeated voice, "I have to leave, don't I?"

I wrap my arms around her. "No, sweetheart, no, you don't have to leave. At least, not all alone. I was thinking maybe we'd leave together."

My proposing I accompany her doesn't placate Lil one bit. She pulls away and eyes me like I'm about to toss her world into turmoil—which, in a way, I guess I am. Still, I insist, "It won't be that bad, Lily."

I'm trying to sound reassuring, but she's not buying it. "I like it *here*, Daddy," she says. "I don't want to go away."

"I know. But we can come back and visit, okay?"

Her eyes start to water. "I don't want to go. You go. Let me stay with Auntie Kay and Uncle Chase. Or I go live with Mommy Emma. I love her so much, Daddy."

I want to say I love Emma too, but I'm currently too stunned that Lily just called her "Mommy Emma." Usually it's Miss Emma, never Mommy Emma.

Wow. This has to stop.

Why? I don't know. But then again, maybe it's because Lily's words make me realize how much Emma has become a part of our lives. She *is* like a mom to Lily. And what a dick I'll be if I accept this New York job offer and leave this good life in the dust, this new life I've been building with Emma.

In a sharp tone, one brought on more by my own frustration and guilt, I snap, "Emma is not your mommy, Lily."

Bad move. All that does is make my daughter burst out in tears.

"I don't have *any* mommy," she cries. "We're leaving Mommy Emma, and my real mommy left me. My real mommy hates me. And Mommy Emma's gonna hate me, too."

"That's not true, Lily. Emma loves you, and your real mommy cares for you too, in her own weird way."

"No! My mommy hates me," Lily screeches.

I try to comfort my daughter, but she pushes me away. "And I hate *you*!" she yells.

"Lily, don't say that."

"I do, Daddy. I hate you. You make us go away, and I hate you, I hate you!"

I let her yell and scream at me. I deserve it.

Lily calms after a while, but she still won't let me comfort her. Defeated, I head to the kitchen so I can make breakfast since I'm canceling with Emma.

Speaking of which… I grab my cell.

I try to keep the ensuing call short, but Emma suspects something. She asks me as much as I am about to hit *End*.

"What's really going on here, Will?"

"Nothing," I say.

"Hey, it's me you're talking to. You can share stuff with me. You know this, right?"

I sigh and rake my fingers through my hair. She's right, but I can't share *this* with her. Not now, not after breaking the news to Lily and with how poorly she took it.

Nevertheless, I say, "I know, Emma."

Just then, Lily starts bawling, really loudly, and I say in a hurry, "I have to go."

I end the call, go to Lily. She pushes me away, again.

"Fine," I say. "I was about to make us some breakfast, anyway. Maybe after you eat you'll feel better."

She ignores me.

Fifteen minutes later, I bring in Lily's breakfast on a small tray. "How 'bout breakfast in bed for my little princess?"

She flops on her stomach and says, "No," as she buries her face in the pillows.

"Lily." I walk over to her bed and set the tray down gently on the edge. "Come on," I prompt in a sing-song voice. "I made your favorite, a sunny-side-up egg."

No response.

I shift my weight and fold my arms across my chest. "There's orange juice, too," I add. "Yum, yum."

Lil loves orange juice, and I guess I'm hoping my thoughtfulness to include a big glass of the stuff might soften her up.

She rolls over on her back, but refuses to make eye contact. Instead, she stares up at the skylight in the ceiling. "I'm not going," she states.

"Lily," I say on a sigh. "If I go, you have to go."

"No, I don't."

"Yes, you do."

"No, no, no!" She starts kicking and thrashing about, and next thing I know the tray goes flying, leaving me covered in yolk and OJ.

"Lily, what the f—" I catch myself, and go instead with a stern, "You're going to clean this mess up, little miss."

Lily shoots me an expression that clearly states: *Yeah, right.*

In the end, she wins. I give in and clean the mess myself.

Fuck. I can't discipline my daughter, I can't make anyone happy, and I can't do anything right.

Later that morning, when Lily asks if she can go next door to play with Sarah, I say in a defeated tone, "Yeah, sure, okay."

Frankly, I'm mentally exhausted. It's probably good for Lily to go play and forget about her rough morning, courtesy of my surprise announcement. However, I don't take into account that my daughter is smart for five. She's seen too much for her young age, and she's not above doing whatever she has to in order to feel back in control.

I realize all this ten minutes later when Chase shows up at my place.

"What's up, bro?" I ask as he walks in without knocking.

I initially assume he's here to ask me to run to town with him, or some such shit where we can hang and shoot the breeze.

That assumption is blown out of the water when Chase levels me with a *what-the-fuck* stare and asks, "What's this I hear about you moving?"

Shit. Busted.

THIRTY-FOUR

Will

I EXPLAIN everything to Chase, and he sure as hell looks disappointed. Nonetheless, he doesn't berate me or try to change my mind. I think he knows how hard this decision is for me.

I don't know if it's him I'm trying to convince, or myself, when I say, "I just want what's ultimately best for Lily."

Chase asks, "And you think monetary success fits that bill?"

It's not a snide comment; he seems to genuinely want to know.

After thinking it over, I say, "I think part of being a good father is providing for your kid, yes. You do it, Chase. You work really hard to give your family a good life."

"I try," he replies. "But don't forget, I have Kay. She's always there to pick up the slack when I'm not around.

And vice versa. We're a team." He sighs. "It's a lot tougher on your own."

His steely blue eyes pin me down, and I know he thinks Emma could be the one for me.

But, how will I ever know if I leave?

"Dude," I say on a sigh. "Don't do this to me. Not today, okay?"

Chase scrubs his hand down his face. "Okay, Will, okay." And then he asks, "So, what's next?"

I blow out a breath. "I have to meet with the head of advertising tomorrow. I guess I'll leave in the morning. I gotta drive up to Chicago. This guy who wants to meet me will be there for a conference that starts Monday. The meeting's just a formality, according to the recruiter. Guess the company just wants to make sure I don't have three heads or something."

"When would you start?" Chase asks quietly.

"Late next week, or the following. Though I'll have to head up to New York and get settled in before that."

"Just like you were planning to do back in June?"

"Yeah. Like then."

Shit, I feel like I'm going backwards here.

"Does Mom still have that hotel room reserved for you?" Chase asks.

I nod once. "Yeah, I never canceled it."

Realization dawns on my brother's face. "You kept the room so she'd think you were in New York City, working at your new job, this whole time."

I admit, "Yeah, I didn't want to have to tell her why I was staying in Harmony Creek."

Chase gives me a look. "She's going to find out about Lily eventually, Will."

"I know, man. But not yet, okay? She and Greg are still on that cruise. Just let Mom enjoy her time away, okay?"

"Sure. But she'll be back any day now," Chase reminds

me.

"I'll tell her, I promise. Just not with all this shit going on."

Visions of our overly dramatic mom fill my thoughts, making me cringe.

"What is it?" Chase asks.

Running my hand through my hair, I reply, "I just know the first thing Mom's going to want to do is meet Lily."

"I'm sure she will," my brother agrees.

"Which is fine," I go on. "But only once things settle down. I have enough on my plate at the moment."

"Hey, your secret's safe with me."

"Thanks, bro."

I trust Chase implicitly. He'd never betray me. And really, truth be told, he's been incredible since the day I first showed up at his doorstep with Lily. I tell him as much, and he gives me a bro-hug, patting me on the back real hard.

"You're doing okay, Will. You're great with Lily, and that's really all that matters. Whatever you decide, I'm with you, okay?"

"Thanks, Chase. That means a lot. Really, it does."

It's true. My brother's support means more than he could ever know.

THIRTY-FIVE

Emma

ON Sunday, I skip church. I do, however, slip into the school to get some work done.

I'm hoping to be left alone, but that doesn't happen. Kay and Chase show up in my classroom around noon. All the kids are with them, including Lily. Funny that there's no sign of Will.

Whatever. I'm tired of worrying about what's up with him.

It takes me a few seconds to realize this is no social call. Kay's holding a cloth up to Jack's nose, which is bleeding.

Rushing over, I ask, "What happened?"

Sarah giggles. "I kick Jack in nose when he help me tie my shoe."

My eyes meet Kay's. "It was an accident," she says.

"We think," Chase interjects.

Kay shoots him a look. "Anyway, we need to take Jack to the hospital to make sure his nose isn't broken. Can you watch the girls?"

"Sure," I reply.

I'm dying to ask where Will is, seeing as one of the girls I'm about to keep an eye on is Lily. But before I have a chance to ask anything, Chase, Kay, and Jack are out the door.

Turning to Sarah and Lily, I say, "So, what would you little ladies like to do?"

They shrug simultaneously.

"Want to color?" I ask.

Lily is up for that, but Sarah has other ideas.

"I no want to color. That's boring. Let's go play outside," she says.

"Well, let me see..." I look around the classroom, noting that most of my work is done. "I guess we could go outside for a while."

"Can we swing on the swings?" Lily wants to know.

Crap. How in the hell does she know about the swings? Will must have told her there's an old swing set down in the woods behind the school.

"Oh, I don't know," I say, wary.

"Yes, swing, swing! I wanna swing," Sarah adds as she spins in a circle.

She sure is wound up today. That's probably why Jack got hurt.

Lily joins in the spinning game, and when she encourages Sarah to spin faster and faster, I start to question who wound up whom. Lily seems to really be acting out, and I have to wonder if it has something to do with Will's absence today.

"Okay, girls, enough." I get them under control. Well, mostly. "Let's go outside."

My declaration is met with cheers, and more calls of, "We go swing on the swing set."

"I don't know about that," I reply.

But after five more minutes of pleas to see the swings, the girls wear me down.

Leading them down to the swing set in the woods, we trudge over a steep embankment, making me glad I wore jeans and Chucks today and nothing fancy.

Once we reach the clearing, Lily immediately jumps up on one of the intact wooden seats. Sarah slowly climbs up on the other.

As I lean against a tree to keep an eye on the girls, I remind them, "Be careful. No swinging too high or too fast."

Sarah is not a worry; she can't muster enough momentum to go very high at all. But Lily is a different story. She's a little taller and easily uses her feet to kick off the ground repeatedly. In no time at all, she is swinging way too high. So high, in fact, that the chains on her swing begin to make creaking and cracking sounds.

Stepping over to the swings, but being careful not to get hit by one, I urge Lily, "Hey, slow down some."

"Nooooo," she replies as she soars even higher.

Sarah slows to a complete stop and twists around so she can watch Lily fly through the air. "Illy, be careful," she says.

Lily doesn't heed either of our warnings. She keeps swinging—high, high, higher—leaving my heart lodged in my throat.

"Lily, seriously, you better slow down right now!"

Blonde hair flying, Lily giggles as she peers down at me. With dirt smudges on her lavender leggings and top, and soaring as she is, almost touching the leaves on the trees around her, she looks like some kind of little wood elf.

When she finally starts to slow, I smile. Crisis averted. Still, Will's little girl is full of mischief, much like her father. One thing for sure, nothing is ever boring with those two.

Just then, when all appears to be under control, a slow wood-cracking sound fills the air.

Sarah looks up at Lily, who, though not nearly as high as before, is still in mid-flight. "Uh-oh," Sarah murmurs.

Before I even realize what's happening, Lily's wooden swing seat breaks in two, sending Lily flying to the ground in a motionless heap.

THIRTY-SIX

Will

S OMETIME around noon, while on my way to Chicago, the weirdest feeling washes over me.

Here comes the turmoil that's been absent from my life, my gut tells me.

This new sense of dread is not unlike the impending doom I felt before Cassie showed up with Lily. But this time it's far more intense, a sharp stab of loss, not a dull nagging like before. I actually have to slow the car and pull over at a rest stop on the side of the interstate.

"Jesus." I take a few deep breaths to calm my racing heart. "What the hell?"

Just then, my cell phone rings.

Grabbing it up from the seat next to me, and expecting the worst, my vision blurs. When I can finally make out Chase's name on the screen, I definitely know this can't be good.

"Chase," I gasp out as I answer. "Jesus, I know

something is wrong. Please, just tell me Lily is all right"

"Will," my brother utters on a pained sigh. "You need to turn around and come back to Harmony Creek as soon as you can."

Panic rises, pulling my voice taut as a rope. "Chase, is Lily okay?" Silence, and then I'm yelling in the phone, "Chase! Jesus, man, tell me my daughter is okay."

"There's been an accident, Will—"

I start backing out of the parking space and almost slam into a passing car. "Asshole," someone yells.

"Fuck you!" I shout back.

"Will, calm down," I hear Chase say.

I don't even realize I dropped the phone.

Shaking my head, and scooping my cell up from the floorboard, I say as evenly as I can, "What kind of accident? Please tell me Lily is fine." My throat constricts, and I can barely add, "Where is she, Chase? Where's my little girl?"

I've never felt emotions like these—helplessness, despair—as deeply as I do right now. There's a lump lodged in my throat and I'm sweating, yet I'm cold.

"What happened? What happened?" I whisper, over and over.

Chase tries to calm me with words and an explanation, but the fucking phone starts breaking up and all I hear are bits and pieces.

"Fell off... swing... hospital... Lily... unconscious."

And then we're disconnected for good.

"Fuck!" I throw the phone, and it bounces off the console and lands on the passenger-side seat.

I drive back to Harmony Creek like a maniac. When I reach the only hospital in town, assuming it has to be the one Lily has been admitted to, I careen into the lot, tires squealing, and screech into a parking spot like I'm some cop on a TV show.

And then it's all flashes, nothing clear.

I'm in the emergency room.

Chase is in the hall.

Kay is next to him.

And Emma is there, as well.

Wait, what's she doing here?

Ah, she's keeping an eye on Jack and Sarah in the waiting area. Jack has a bandage on his nose, but looks more or less fine. Maybe he was involved in the same accident, and Lily will come out any minute with just a bandage on her cute little nose, too.

"Where's Lily?" I ask when Chase meets me halfway down the corridor.

"Hey, I want you to calm down, okay? Flipping out is not going to do anyone any good."

What? Is he kidding? "Where's my fucking daughter, Chase?"

Two nurses walk by and give us tense looks. I realize then that Chase has his hands on my shoulders. He's holding me back. "They're checking her over, okay?" he says.

"Is she going to be okay?" My voice cracks.

"We think so," Chase replies, and I almost collapse in his arms. He holds me steady, and adds, "They won't tell us much, though. And only a parent or guardian can go in and see her."

Shit, this is bad.

I push past my brother, but then it's Emma blocking my way. "Get out of the way," I grind out.

I'm not trying to be mean, but I don't have time for whatever it is she may want to talk about, which is probably why I haven't called her since yesterday morning when I blew her off for breakfast. But when I see tears in Emma's eyes, and notice her nose is red like she's been crying, I lighten up. I remind myself she cares for Lily, too.

"Look," I say, much more kindly, "we can talk later. I

need to see Lily right now."

She starts to cry. "I know, I know. But I have to tell you that I'm sorry, Will. I am so, so sorry. I told Lily not to go too high. And then she was coming down, and…and the swing broke and—"

This is fucking unbelievable. "What? You were with my daughter when this happened?"

"Yes," she whispers.

I shake my head. "You took my girl to play on those old, rusty swings, didn't you?" She barely nods, and I go off. "What the hell were you thinking? Did you do this because you were mad at me?"

"What? No!"

Emma appears shocked. And, truly, I can barely believe myself that I'm spouting off like this.

Chase, sensing I'm about to implode, grabs my arm. "Hey, come on. Let's go see Lily."

I shrug him off me and take a step closer to Emma. "Get the fuck out of here," I hiss. "I don't want you around my daughter."

She tries to touch me, and I jerk away. "Will, please—"

"Seriously, Emma, just go."

I would never lay a hand on any woman, but I'm so mad at Emma I *do* feel like screaming some very nasty things at her. Truthfully, however, all this anger is misdirected. I'm mad at myself for leaving Lily. Emma is an easy target because, for as far as I've come, it's still too easy to revert back to my old asshole behaviors. It's simpler than dealing with the guilt.

Chase pulls Emma aside and tells her, much more kindly than I, that she should probably leave. She nods and blinks back tears as she tries to catch my eye.

Pushing past them both, I go to find my daughter.

THIRTY-SEVEN

Emma

I LEAVE the hospital and go home.

My apartment has never felt so empty. *I* have never felt so empty. How can Will ever forgive me? I'm not even that mad at him for being angry with me. I deserved some of his ire. I never should have taken Lily and Sarah down to play behind the school on that old, decrepit swing set.

What in the hell was I thinking?

Disappointed in myself—*I'm a teacher, for God's sake, I should know better*—I head to the bathroom to take a shower. Maybe hot water can wash away my remorse.

But even after thirty minutes of standing under almost-scalding hot water, and with my skin as pink as hell, my heart remains heavy. Releasing a pent-up breath, I hop out of the shower, dry off, and then slip on a short robe made of white silk. Five minutes later, I am curled up on the sofa.

All I want to do is doze off and forget this day ever happened.

Finding peace is easier said than done. My mind insists on replaying the events of the day. They're all bad, too—like when Kay informed me at the hospital that Will was on his way to Chicago for an interview for another job in New York City. When did that come up? Will obviously didn't think I was important enough to call and let know he may be leaving town. I thought this job stuff was decided long ago. Doesn't he realize I love him? And Lily, too? I don't want either of them to go away.

A tear slides down my cheek.

Shit, I told myself I was done crying.

My phone beeps a little while later, and I hastily snatch it up from where it rests on a sofa cushion.

It's not Will, unfortunately.

Rather, it's a text from Kay. *I thought you'd want to know Lily is going to be fine.*

I breathe a sigh of relief and continue reading.

The doctors ran tons of tests, imaging and such. Everything looks good, but they've decided to keep her overnight for observation. Apart from a nasty bump on her head, she seems fine.

Oh, thank God, I type back. *Thank you for thinking of me and letting me know. I was really worried. I just wish I could come see Lily.*

Kay: *Visiting hours just ended. Will's here, of course, and he'll be staying with Lily for a little while longer. The staff made an exception for him, but only for another hour. Anyway, if you need to talk to someone, Emma, I'm here.*

I type back: *Thanks, Kay.*

Despite her kind offer, I don't call. I'm sure Kay wants to spend this time with her own children, before she puts them to bed. Jack has had a tough day, as well, though not as rough as Lily's. His nose will be fine. There was no break, just lots of swelling.

A little over an hour after receiving Kay's text, there's a frenzy of knocks on my apartment door. I am thrown into an internal debate as to whether I should acknowledge the individual knocking, since I have a strong suspicion I know precisely who it is.

Sure enough, following several more insistent raps, Will's voice rings out from outside.

"Emma, please," I hear him plead. "I know I've been the biggest prick lately, especially over at the hospital, and I'm sorry, I am." Another knock rings out, and I can almost feel his desperation. "Please, Emma, please let me in so we can talk about this."

I can't in good conscience continue to ignore him, so I go to the door and let him in.

Without a word from either of us, Will walks into my apartment, slowly, his steps as pained as the expression on his face. He's sorry for how he behaved, I can tell. Still, with his nasty dismissal of me at the hospital, and his assuming the worst, I don't know if I can forgive him instantly.

Clearing my throat, I say, "I heard from Kay. She said Lily is going to be fine." I blow out a breath. "That's certainly good news."

Will scrubs a hand down his face. "Yes, it is, it is. Just... Thank God." Suddenly choking out another apology, he reaches for me.

But I take a step back. "Will, I don't know."

"Emma, please."

I give in then, allowing him to encircle me in his arms. "Fuck, Emma," he says. "I am so, so, so sorry for flipping out on you. I wasn't really mad at you. I was pissed at myself."

I remain tense, at first, but Will's warm body pressed to mine feels so good, so right, so comforting. And I can't help it—I love him no matter what.

When I start to relax, he tightens his arms around me. "I'm sorry for the things I said to you. I wish I could take them back."

"Will, let's not..." I trail off, not sure what I want to say.

"Look," he begins, "here's the problem. I have a bad habit of pushing blame to the people I love the most. It's wrong, and I know it. And I swear I'm trying to stop that shit. But sometimes, Emma, sometimes I slip."

"You weren't completely in the wrong," I allow.

When I lean back and am able to see his face, I see he's shaking his head. "No, no, I'm the dick in this equation," he insists.

"Okay, maybe a little," I grant him, smiling slightly. "But you were right about one thing—I never should have taken the girls down to that old swing set."

"Maybe, but I was wrong to tell Lily about it in the first place," Will counters. "I should've known she'd want to go to any place I tell her about."

"Still, I wasn't thinking, Will."

"Hey." He lifts my chin so I can meet his gaze. Damn, his eyes are so green today. I can't help but lose myself in their depths, till he prompts, "Emma?"

"Yes." I shake my head, and Will's hand moves with me. He doesn't let go, and there's something in that, something that says *I'm here* and *I'm sorry*.

Sighing, Will says quietly, "I'm sorry I didn't tell you about the interview. That was another shit move. I just didn't..." He pauses, reflects. "I guess I was afraid you'd talk me out of it. I know you don't want me to leave."

"I thought it was settled that you were staying?" I croak out.

"I thought so, too," he replies.

"So, what happened?"

"I don't know. I heard from the recruiter, and he made it sound like this would be my last chance, like, *ever*."

Softly, I say, "I really want to support anything you choose to do, but I have to be honest. I don't want you to go. It's not just you I'd be losing; it's your daughter, too. And I love Lily a lot, Will."

"I know, babe, I know." He releases my chin and presses his lips to my forehead. "We both love you, too."

"I'd never stop you from doing what you need to do," I continue, "for yourself, and for Lily."

Peering down at me, he says, "It was still shitty of me to take off and not let you know what was happening."

I tap his chest, the cotton of his light green tee so soft over his hard pecs. "What happens next, then?"

He shrugs. "Well, I spoke with the recruiter on the way over. The company knows I had a family emergency. And it looks like they'll be rescheduling my meeting for this week sometime."

"So, if you get this job, does that mean you'd have to leave before Lily even starts school?"

Closing his eyes, he whispers, "I'm sorry, Emma, but yeah, probably."

"What about us?" I squeak out.

Will opens his eyes and watches his own hand as he skims it down my cheek. "I love you. I don't want this to end. I can tell you that much."

I wait for more. It seems he wants to ask more, too. I want nothing more than for Will to ask me to move to New York with him. But, in the end, he doesn't say anything else.

Swallowing my disappointment, I say, "So, we'd try the long-distance thing?"

"If you think you're up for it, yeah."

It's not what I want, but at this point, I'll take whatever Will is willing to give. If that makes me desperate, so be it.

214 THE AFTER OF US

Love makes all of us desperate in one way or another. It's an unavoidable consequence of placing your fragile heart in another's hands.

"I'm up for trying," I say to Will as I put on a happy face.

And then, for this one long, drawn-out minute I consider whether I should tell him about the agent who asked to see his work. But then, if I fess up to my act, I'll also have to confess that I sent his work without his consent. What if he gets mad? Or, worse yet, what if he doesn't mind at all? What if Will is actually glad I took the initiative?

That all sounds wonderful, until you factor in that the agent's response could very well be a firm rejection letter. Talk about pumping up someone's hopes, just to crush them all to hell.

So, no. In the end, I decide to keep my mouth shut and my secret safe.

Will tilts back my head, and asks, "What's going on in there, Emma?"

His hands in my hair feel possessive, in a way I like. His eyes search mine, searing my soul. I let out a gasp that probably gives me away. But I don't care. Truth is I am putty in Will's hands. I like that he makes me feel this way, so vulnerable. There's something about him that makes me yearn to submit to him. Problem is I know I'll crack and tell him what I'm hiding if I don't submit to him right now in *some* way.

Giving in to a feeling of lust that's bubbling to the surface, I lick my lips and say, "Will, I want you so much right now. I *need* you."

He knows what I'm intimating, and his hold on me tightens. His gaze scans down my body, like he's just realizing how little I have on. I guess, in some ways, Will is putty in my hands, as well.

His eyes find mine, silently requesting permission as he takes hold of the sash that's keeping my robe closed.

"Yes," I tell him.

With one smooth move, he tugs at the sash and it falls away, making my robe gape open. Will takes in my naked body. And then, showing vulnerability of his own, he drops to his knees and rests his cheek against my bare tummy, his warm breaths a teasing caress. His fingers trail up the inside of my thigh, until he reaches where I want him so badly. When I whimper, he gives me more, tracing the building moisture along my slit.

"I need to taste you right now," he rasps.

Knees trembling, I have no adequate reply. And Will doesn't need one. Urging me to widen my stance, he kisses down my abdomen till his tongue touches my swollen clit. It's just a brush at first, but more than enough to make me grow wetter and crave more.

I place my hands on his shoulders to keep from falling, and he licks me again and again, sucking my nub into his mouth with each enthusiastic pass.

"I could fucking lick your pussy all day," he tells me at one point, his voice gruff and raw against my sex.

My knees grow weaker and weaker. "I have to sit down," I reply as my nails dig into his shoulders.

Will helps me to the floor and lays me back gently. I then watch as he whips off his tee, revealing all those hard muscles and ripples I adore.

He keeps stroking me, watching my reactions, and I like it. My pulse races as I shift and impale myself on his fingers. Will pumps in and out of me, and then, when he does the little curling thing I love with his index finger, I fall apart.

Between orgasmic shudders, I breathe out, "Maybe we should take a break?"

"No break," Will says with a chuckle. He nudges

my pliant legs open farther and informs me, "I'm not anywhere near done with you."

I think I'm ready for what he has planned next, but shit, I am so not. Will buries his head between my still-quivering legs and does more sinful things with his tongue. I am licked, sucked, and probed until my whole body is on fire, and all I see when I squeeze my eyes shut is blinding white as I come and come and come.

When I finally drift down from euphoria, I am lying wet and open for Will. Standing over me, he undoes his jeans, and I watch as he takes out and handles his cock.

With lust-hooded eyes and aching for more, I ask, "Is that for me?"

His hand glides up his shaft and crests over the purplish head, spreading a clear drop of liquid. "You want it?" he asks, raising a brow as he peers down at me.

"Uh-huh. And I want to taste you, too," I say, because I really, really do.

Will kneels by my head and nudges my mouth open. He guides his cock in, allowing me to do what I want— taste him, all salty and soapy and so male.

He toys with my nipples while I suck and lick, and when his breathing picks up he skims his hand down to part my lips so he can fuck me with his fingers some more. He then leaves my mouth, and the next thing I know he is pushing at my entrance.

I shift to accommodate him, but Will makes me wait. He toys with me with the head of his cock, a hot drop of cum coating my clit, mixing with my own juices. And, finally, he fills me, stretching me, loving me.

He moves like a piston when he really gets going, his thrusts so wild and frenzied we become like wild beasts. Will fucks me, hard, but I fuck him back just as roughly. I meet his rapid pumps, circling my hips, grabbing his ass.

"Fuck me harder," I grind out in his ear as I dig my

nails into his back. "As hard as you can. You won't hurt me."

Will growls and pushes my legs back as far as he can. He pulls out almost all the way, and we both peer down at our joined bodies. "Fuck, that is hot," he says.

He then slams back into me, again and again, harder each time. He's so deep inside of me that I feel as if he could keep going and tear me in two. And I want that; I need him like this, raw and unrelenting. I need to be taken, as much as Will needs to take me. This is the culmination and release of all my mistakes and his. This is me still holding a secret, and this is him trying to come to terms with his decision to leave.

We are changing, and I can feel it.

And then, I know what this is.

This is the after of us from before, who we were, and who we are becoming.

THIRTY-EIGHT

Will

CAN'T wait to pick Lily up from the hospital the next morning.

I stay over at Emma's the night before. There's no way I am leaving her alone after all that hot sex. But, really, it's more than that. Holding Emma throughout the night—and her holding me—is what we both need.

I guess I'm starting to understand what it means to really be in love. I once thought I loved Cassie, but I know now my feelings for her were immature and greedy. This is vastly different. My love for Emma is deep. It's something undeniable in my soul.

Unfortunately, though I don't *want* to leave her, I may have to. The wheels are back in motion with the job. No more trips to Chicago. The new plan is to fly up to New York City to meet an even higher-level exec this Friday.

Shit, they must really want me.

Do I want them, though?

Does it matter?

If I could go back in time, I'd send out query letters and samples of my work to all those agents. I'd try for my dream. But after what happened with Lily, I'm realizing I can't keep pissing around. I need to make a decision and stick with it.

But what will that decision be?

Something is different, but I can't put my finger on what it is exactly. I just know I feel more like myself than I have in a long time, and I don't want to lose that.

Smiling over at a sleeping Emma, I lean over and deposit a soft kiss on her shoulder. She's part of why I feel so good today. She sometimes brings out the worst in me, but she mostly brings out the best. Maybe she can move to New York with me? Last night, I thought about asking her to come with me. But something made me hold back.

I'll ask her for sure…if I *really* end up going.

I try not to wake Emma, but when I kiss her shoulder again she rouses.

"Oh, crap." She sits up abruptly, the sheet slipping away and exposing her delicious and so-damn-sexy pink, pert nipples. "What time is it? I have to go to work, and you have to pick up Lily."

"Shh, shh. Don't worry, it's really early." I pull her down to my chest, her breasts so warm pressed to me. "In fact, we probably have time to—"

"Say no more." Emma silences me with a deep kiss.

And then she straddles me. She is more than ready for me. Seems we're always so ready for one another.

Damn, I love this girl.

Lily is happy to get out of the hospital. "It smells funny in there," she tells me, complete with a nose scrunch as we drive out of the parking lot.

I can't help but laugh. "It does smell weird, Lil, I know."

When we stop at a red light, I glance back at her in the rearview mirror. She looks great, all things considered. There's a big bump on the back of her head, not visible from my vantage point, but really, Lily is lucky. She took a nasty fall, but came out essentially unscathed.

She smiles at me when she notices me watching her. "Whatcha' thinking about, Daddy?"

"Just how much I love you, honey," I reply.

"Love you, too." She spreads her arms as far as she can. "This much."

"Whoa, that's a lot."

The light turns green and I return to concentrating on the road. But my ears are free, and I'm happy to listen to Lily chattering in the back.

At one point, she asks, "Are we going to stay home now?"

Home. The word hits me hard. This *has* become our home. There's love and family in Harmony Creek. And there's Emma.

I think I knew it last night, and even this morning, but Lily solidifies it for me with those seven little words. No more back-and-forth waffling, no more changing my mind on a whim, no more allowing turmoil that arises in my life — which is inevitable — to misdirect me. I'm taking charge, I'm growing up. I am finally becoming the man I need to be — for Lily, for Emma, and for me.

I pull into a strip mall parking lot, choosing a space far away from the other cars. I'm about to have a discussion too important to allow distractions.

I unbuckle my seatbelt and slip from the driver's seat. When I hop into the back with Lily, I say, "Do you want to stay here in Ohio, Lil?"

She nods. "Yes." Her response is uttered in a level

voice, calm, like a little adult.

"Oh, Lil." I rake my fingers through my hair. "I'm sorry I've been all over the place. I guess I thought I had this crap all figured out. I've always just wanted what's best for you. I want so much to give you a good life…and a father who's successful."

"What's sah-ses-ful?" she asks.

I sigh. "Good question, Lil."

I think about what I've been taught to measure success by these past few years—money and material things. When I was little and my family had money, love always remained the focus. The money was an afterthought, something nice, but not wholly necessary. But after my dad died—and Chase, my mom, and I were destitute—my mom became driven to get us back to the life we once had.

But she never recognized that money can't buy happiness. Sadly, she still can't figure that out. Even after she met Greg—and he's a good dude, don't get me wrong—she could never recapture what we once had. Too much had occurred. We were all changed. Nonetheless, my mom has since tried to make up for what's missing by showering me—and Chase, to a lesser extent—with money and material things.

I look around at the luxurious interior of the car Lily and I are in, this fancy BMW my mother bought me as a graduation gift. I appreciate it, I do, but I don't ever want to become like my mom. I never want to be stuck resorting to showering Lily with material things to make up for not being there for her.

Lily, seeing me shaking my head, reaches over and touches my hand. "Daddy, don't be sad."

I lean over and give her a hug, albeit an awkward one with the car seat straps in the way. "Aw, sweetie, I'm not sad. I'm just thinking about things."

When I settle back next to her, she asks, "What kinda

things you think 'bout now?"

I need not explain how I'm reviewing in my mind what to say to the recruiter I'll be calling when I get home, like how I plan to tell him to cancel the interview, permanently.

I have a new goal—fulfilling my dream. I'll freelance in the meantime, build up my name, and work for Chase on the side. It'll have to be enough.

Lily doesn't need all those details, though, so I simply smile over at her and say, "I'm thinking you're right. We should stay right where we are."

Her emerald eyes—*my* eyes—fill with hope. "We stay here with Uncle Chase and Auntie Kay?"

She's making sure, and I nod enthusiastically. "Yes, Lily, we're staying right here with Uncle Chase and Aunt Kay."

"With Sarah and Jack, too?"

"Yes, we'll be here with them, too."

"Good."

Since I'm striving to be completely honest, I'm careful to add, "We may not live over in the garage apartment forever, Lil. We'll probably get our own place someday."

Lily's eyes widen. "Wow, Daddy. You mean, like, our very own house?"

I can't help but smile, as she's so serious. "Yes, Lil, our very own house."

She then blurts out, "Can Mommy Emma come live with us, too?"

She shoots me a wide-eyed, *uh-oh* expression, probably recalling how I, like the ass I can be, told her not to call Emma her mommy.

Quickly, Lily amends, "I mean Miss Emma."

I place my hand on her little shoulder and squeeze. "Hey, Lily, I don't mind if you want to call Emma 'Mommy Emma.'"

Quietly, she asks, "You think maybe someday she

want to be my mommy, like, o-fiss-olly?"

For the first time, I feel no panic, no uncertainty, at that prospect. Truth is I want Emma to remain in our lives, as much as, if not more so than, Lily does.

Leaning over to kiss Lily's cheek, I murmur, "Maybe, sweetheart, maybe."

THIRTY-NINE

Emma

A T daycare on Monday, I check my email—from my phone—every chance I get. I'm hoping to hear back from the agent I sent Will's complete comic book manuscript to.

There's no reply at eleven. And still nothing through lunchtime.

Nothing, as well, during afternoon naptime for the kids.

And *still* nothing at three thirty.

Dammit!

A few of the early parents arrive to pick up their kids. And then the rest come.

My email remains empty.

And then I am at home, strolling through the door of my apartment.

My phone dings as I kick off my heels, indicating that I have a voicemail. I check it hastily and find it's from Will.

As I listen to his voicemail, I sense excitement in his

tone.

Hey, babe. Hope your day's been as good as mine. Lily's doing great, by the way. After I picked her up at the hospital, we spent the whole day together. We hung out at home, like the doctor recommended, just taking it easy. Of course, Lily wanted to color and draw, since running around outside was out. He pauses, and then chuckles. *I think my hand might fall off from all the drawing she had me do. Anyway, can I see you tonight? I have something I want to share with you. I'll be over at seven, if that's okay? If that's not good, just shoot me a text. Shit, I can't wait to see you, babe.*

There's no hint or indication of what this "something" Will wants to share with me could be. I'm excited to find out, but disappointed I have no good news for him.

Before getting ready for Will's impending visit, I nuke a microwave meal and devour it in all of about ten minutes. I then take a quick shower, slip on a cute pair of white shorts and a royal blue V-neck tee, and settle in to wait for Will.

Hunkering down on the sofa, I check my email for what has to be the fiftieth time.

And this time... "Holy crap, the agent replied!"

I read the email carefully. And then I re-read it two more times to make sure my eyes aren't deceiving me. But, no, I read it correctly the first time, and here's the gist— the agent *loves* Will's work. In fact, she's so impressed she wants to speak with him on the phone about turning his comic book into a graphic novel—like he's dreamed of— as soon as possible.

That's it—I have to tell him tonight. Maybe he'll even decide to stay after hearing this good news.

A girl can dream, right?

Will arrives at seven, and I let him in.

When I can't quit smiling, he asks, "What has you so happy?"

I give him a hug. "You," I reply.

"Oh, yeah?"

"Yep."

He looks pretty damn happy himself, so I add, "You seem happy, too. Looks like both our days have been awesome."

He narrows the gap between us and leans down so our lips are close. "Let's make things even better."

He then kisses me.

And after a truly breathtaking kiss — Will's an amazing kisser — I murmur, "Wow. Do you think I'll ever get tired of those lips of yours?"

Chuckling, he says, "I hope not." Leading me over to the sofa, he adds, "Anyway, like I mentioned in the voicemail, I have something I need to tell you."

On the coffee table in front of the sofa lies the printout of the agent's response, the one I can't wait to share with Will.

But not yet.

When I sit down, I snatch up the letter so Will doesn't see it before I have a chance to explain how it came to be.

With the letter grasped in my hand, blank-side up, I say, "I actually have something to share with you, too."

Will takes a seat beside me. "Okay," he says, glancing at the letter. "Is that it?"

"Yes. And I hope you won't be mad when you see what's on it."

He suddenly looks panicked as he asks, "Why would I be mad over what's on a piece of paper?"

Poor guy probably thinks it's a positive pregnancy test result after having been blindsided by Cassie. But he needn't be concerned; that's well covered on my end.

"It's nothing bad," I assure him. "In fact, it's great news. I just don't want you to hate me for going behind your back." I pause, and then say, "Just know I did this with the best intentions. I only want you to be happy, Will."

In a low voice, complete with a *melt-me-now* smile, Will says, "I *am* happy, Emma."

I start to hand him the agent's letter, but he stills my hand. "Wait. Let me tell you my news first."

"Okay."

He inhales deeply, exhales slowly, and then blurts out in a rush, "I'm staying, Emma. Right here in Harmony Creek. New York—or any other city, for that matter—is permanently out. You're stuck with me now, babe."

I twist to face him more fully. "What? No way! Will, this really is amazing news."

Joy and relief wash over me, and all I want to do is tackle him and hug him like crazy. But I have to restrain myself and wait for him to finish.

"It's true, I'm staying." He smiles over at me. "I called the recruiter and cancelled everything. No more back and forth crap, I promise. I'm making a commitment, Emma, to *you*. And I know in doing so that I'm also doing what's best for my daughter."

Now I *have* to hug him, it's no longer a choice.

The piece of paper falls from my hand and ends up smooshed between our bodies. "Oh, wait."

I pull back so I can retrieve the crumpled letter.

"What the hell is on that thing, anyway?" Will wants to know.

Instead of going through the whole story, I simply hand it to him.

He looks down at the letter, murmuring three shocked "wows" as he reads. When he's done, he doesn't look up. He just stares down at the paper.

"You're mad, aren't you?" I say softly.

Will shakes his head, but his lips are pressed together in a tight line. I don't know what to think.

"Will, please, say something," I implore.

I watch as he swallows hard. But still, he remains quiet.

Sighing heavily, and suspecting a grim response, despite the shake of his head, I try to explain. "I know I shouldn't have gone behind your back. But Will, your work is so damn good. And I was so afraid you'd given up on pursuing what you once told me was your dream—"

"It *is* my dream, Emma. Not was."

Though he's speaking now, his gaze remains on the letter.

But then he looks over at me, and his greens are wet with unshed tears. "I'm not mad you took the initiative," he tells me. "I'm just stunned that after all the shit I put you through, you still cared enough about me to do something like this."

In a whisper, I reply, "It's because I love you, Will Gartner. With all my heart, and all my soul, I love you, you stubborn man."

FORTY

Will

A<small>ND</small> right there, with those words, Emma shows me what love really is.

"I love you, too," I tell her as I wrap my arms around her.

And then I promise what I know she needs to hear. "I will always stay with you, Emma. You are my and Lily's future."

She chokes up, but behind the tears, there is joy. "Oh, Will."

Emma leans her head on my shoulder, and I hold her close to me. We stay like that for a long time, merely content with one another's presence. It was always so simple, this answer I sought. How could I not have seen it sooner?

I'm what Emma needs, and she's it for me. Who knew I'd discover what I needed all along was right here in Harmony Creek the whole time?

Life certainly works in mysterious ways sometimes.

The next couple of weeks are a whirlwind of activity, all of it good. Emma and I take Lily school shopping with the big first day looming.

The night before kindergarten is set to begin, I ask Lily, "You ready for your first day of real school?"

"Uh-huh."

We're gathered in Chase and Kay's living room, with my brother and his wife. Emma is here too, and Jack and Sarah, of course.

Jack, reveling in his one-grade-ahead status, assures Lily, "Don't worry. Lily. I'll watch out for you."

Chase pats his son approvingly on the head. "That's my boy."

Not to be outdone, Sarah pipes in with, "I take care of you too, Illy."

That prompts Kay to applaud Sarah for her own protective streak. "That's *my* girl," she says, side-eyeing Chase.

Chase and I burst out laughing.

Laughing is something I seem to do a lot more of these days. And why wouldn't I? Life is good, really good.

And it just keeps getting better.

After speaking with the agent who liked my work, I ended up signing a really great deal with a big publisher and a big advance. It's not enough money to give up freelancing completely, but I can cut down on my hours working for Chase.

"Concentrate on your future, bro," Chase said when I inked the deal. "Just know if you ever need the extra work, it's here."

I thanked him, as it's always wise to have a backup

plan to fill in the unexpected gaps.

Another thing Chase helped me with was my preparation to finally break the news to our mother that I have a daughter.

"She's not going to be mad," he kept assuring me. "You're not a teenage kid anymore."

"I know, I know," I'd reply. "I just hope she forgives me for not calling her as soon as I found out."

"That's the last thing she's going to be worried about, Will."

Chase turned out to be right. When I made the dreaded call, just a few days ago, Abby wasn't even angry. She wasn't even mad about me not taking the job in New York City. She was too overjoyed with the news of Lily to feel any disappointment that I scrapped the business-man plan.

After learning about Lily, and taking a moment to digest it all, my mother's first words were, "That's it. I'm checking my schedule and flying out to Ohio to meet my granddaughter. I want to come as soon as possible. When would be a good time?"

Since I have Chase backing me, not to mention Emma's full support, I told my mother, "Anytime you want, Mom."

We currently have a date set for her to visit in late September.

When I let Lily know she'll be meeting my mom — her grandmother — real soon, she asked me, "What about my other nana? What happen to her?"

She meant Cassie's mom. Mrs. Sutter watched Lily for a long time when Cassie was MIA, so it was no surprise to learn Lily still thinks about her.

"Do you miss your other nana?" I asked her.

She nodded. "Sometimes I do"

I decided then and there to hire a private investigator to search for Lily's maternal grandmother.

I'd like to talk with Cassie's mom anyway, to see what we can do about getting Cassie into rehab. I don't *ever* plan on giving Lily back, but if Cass cleaned up her act, I'd consider letting her see her daughter from time to time. I know it'd be in Lily best interest if she could have her real mom in her life.

Before all that can happen, however, I need one thing to be official—I want full custody of Lily.

The next day, I hire a second PI to find Cassie in Las Vegas, so she can sign over full custody to me. I'm not taking any chances that, on a whim, Cassie may have an urge to snatch Lily away from me.

That is just not *ever* going to happen.

A week later, I get good news. The PI has found Cassie rather easily, and—surprise, surprise—she's signed the papers, no questions asked.

"How was she?" I ask the investigator when he returns with the signed documents.

"Strung out," he tells me.

"How bad was it?"

"Pretty bad."

I shake my head.

A few days later, the first private eye I hired calls in to inform me he has located Cassie's mother. Mrs. Sutter lives in Denver these days.

When I give her a call, and after she expresses great shock to hear from me after all these years, she tentatively asks if I know about Lily.

"Yes," I tell her. "Cassie finally told me."

"I'm sorry I never looked you up and told you," she says, sounding bereft.

Sighing, I say, "Water under the bridge."

Fighting back tears, she asks, "Do you happen to know where Lily is? I know Cassie returned to Nevada with her, but I haven't heard from my daughter in months. She called me once, a long time ago, but I couldn't understand a word of what she was going on and on about. When I tried to call her back, the number she called from had been disconnected."

I let Mrs. Sutter know that Lily is safe and with me, and then I inform her, "I have full custody now."

She releases a relieved breath. "Oh, thank God, Will. Just, thank God." Tentatively, she adds, "Would it be all right if I fly out to Ohio to see Lily sometime?"

"I think Lily would love that," I reply softly.

We then discuss the situation with Cassie.

"I know where she is, at least for the moment," I tell Mrs. Sutter. "If you want to talk to your daughter, I can give you a working number."

"Thank you, Will," she says.

We agree to work together to try and talk Cassie into going back to rehab.

Mrs. Sutter warns me, though, "Don't get your hopes up, Will. Cassie's been down this rehab road so many times. And, unfortunately, for all involved, my daughter always goes back to a life with drugs. If having Lily couldn't keep her sober, I don't know what ever will."

"Still," I maintain, "we have to try."

But when Mrs. Sutter flies to Vegas, after Cassie agrees to visit and talk with her, Cassie bails on the meeting. She then disappears completely from the radar. Deeper into the druggie life, I fear.

"That could've been me," I say to Emma one evening, after informing her that Cassie's gone MIA.

We're out to dinner, on our weekly date night, a routine made possible when Chase and Kay are available to babysit Lily.

From across the table, Emma says softly, "Don't say that, Will. You never would've gotten to that point."

I've told Emma everything, including all the unsavory

details from my past, and she still accepts me for me. *Amazing*.

"Do you know how much I appreciate you being in my life?" I say, changing the subject.

"Will, stop."

She blushes, and I have to laugh. I'm always gushing over Emma these days. I love doting on her, to the point where she's at a loss for words. It's cute when she gets all flustered by the flattery I bestow on her. I just want to make sure she knows how committed I am to her. I feel like I jerked her around way too much the first couple of months of our relationship.

Well, not anymore. Emma now gets the full-on *I'm-completely-in-love-with-you* version of Will.

"It's true," I continue. "With you in my life, I'm finally the man I always wanted to be."

"The man you always wanted to be was there all along," she says.

"Still, you helped me find him, babe."

After dinner, we head back to my place. Not to have sex—we have *a lot* of that, trust me. No, tonight, we're planning a quiet end-of-evening spent with Lil.

After we pick up my daughter at the farmhouse, the three of us begin the short walk over to my apartment. Along the way, Lily tells us all about some old board games she and Sarah found in the attic of the farmhouse. She then proceeds to tell us how they also came upon a "big, scary spider" in one of the dusty boxes.

"Jack brave. He caught it and set it free out a window," Lily informs us.

"Oh, that Jack, he sure is a hero," Emma teases. "I bet Uncle Chase was proud as could be."

"He was p-woud," Lily replies excitedly. "He say Jack saved us."

"Ah, saving damsels in distress," I interject. "Something

we Gartner men are good at doing. It's great to hear Jack's getting a head start on the family legacy."

Lily loses interest in my blustering and runs ahead, leaving me alone with Emma.

Bumping her hip to mine, Emma says flirtatiously, "Hmm, you've been known to save me a few times here and there, Will Gartner."

"Oh, is that so?"

"Uh-huh."

"Well, you, my love, do the same for me. Like, every fucking day of my life."

It's true, Emma does save me. She grounds me, keeps me on course.

In my living room, all three of us curl up on the couch and pick out a movie to watch. Well, Lil picks out the movie. Doesn't matter that it's the same cartoon flick I've seen a dozen times already with her. What matters is that I'm watching this show with my daughter and Emma.

When the movie ends, Lily takes my hand. And then she picks up Emma's hand.

Pressing our hands together, with hers wedged in the middle, she says, "I love you, Daddy."

"I love you too, sweetheart."

Turning to Emma, she states, "I love you too, Mommy."

Emma's eyes flicker to mine as she replies, "Love you too, Lily."

This is the first time Lily has ever left off "Emma" when calling her "Mommy." I nod and let Emma know with my eyes that I'm fine with Lily referring to her as her mom. She's certainly a better mother to my daughter than her biological mom has been, and that's what matters.

After clearing my throat, I say, "Hey, Lil, I have an idea."

"What, Daddy?"

My eyes meet Emma's, and with our hands still

entwined, I say, "What do you think about Mommy moving in with us?"

Emma's bright blues widen. "Really, Will?"

"Yes. If it's okay with you and Lil?"

"Of course it's okay," she whispers, smiling. "It's more than okay."

"So, what do you think, Lily?" I ask, peering down at my smiling daughter. "You okay with that plan, too?"

Lily nods enthusiastically. "Yes, yes! I want Mommy with us all the time." And then, looking at Emma, and then at me, she asks, "Are we a family now, Daddy?"

"Yes, Lily, we sure are."

I guess what they say is true—dreams really can come true.

EPILOGUE

Will

A LL my dreams have come true, and I count myself a lucky man.

Emma moved in with Lily and me a week after the decision to do so was made. And a couple of months later, we bought a small ranch house together. Not far from Chase and Kay and the kids, our new home is located on a nice piece of land, with lots of room for Lily to play.

Unfortunately, Cassie is still not in Lily's life. She resurfaced, and I tried to make her see reason — her mother tried, too — but nothing we said or did got through to her.

Maybe someday things will change.

Lily, thank God, thrives regardless. She no longer asks about her "real" mother. As far as she's concerned, she has a father and mother who love her, and two grandmothers who fly out to see her — and spoil the hell out of her — every chance they get.

And then there's me.

I've grown a lot since finding out about Lily. My daughter showing up in my life helped me discover the life I was truly meant to lead. It sure is funny how things like that work, but work it did for me.

And there's more...

By finally following my true passion—authoring graphic novels—my one-time dream has become my career.

By finally trusting my instincts, I've become a really good father to Lily.

And by finally opening my heart, I found love with Emma.

So, what have I learned?

I've learned that sometimes you have to take a chance, follow your heart, and stop fighting that which is meant to be.

Let your dreams lead you to the happiness you deserve.

The End

About the Author

S.R. Grey is an Amazon Top 100 and Barnes & Noble #1 Bestselling author. She is the author of the popular Judge Me Not series, the new Promises series, the Inevitability duology, A Harbour Falls Mystery trilogy, and the Laid Bare series of novellas. Ms. Grey's works have appeared on several Amazon Bestseller lists, including Top 100 multiple times, as well as #1 on Barnes & Noble Bestselling Nook books list.

Ms. Grey resides in Pennsylvania. When not writing, Ms. Grey can be found reading, traveling, running, or cheering for her hometown sports teams.

Author Website:
srgrey.com

S.R. Grey Facebook:
www.facebook.com/SRGrey

Sign up for S.R. Grey's exclusive-content newsletter and never miss an update, cover reveal, or release:
mad.ly/signups/106801/join

Follow S.R. Grey on Twitter:
twitter.com/AuthorSRGrey

Find blog posts on the S.R. Grey Goodreads Author page:
www.goodreads.com/author/show/6433082.S_R_Grey

Follow S.R. Grey on Instagram:
instagram.com/authorsrgrey#

Acknowledgements

Thank you to everyone who sent me messages, rallying for Will's story to be told. This story is for you, and I hope I did it justice. Also, a huge shout-out to my street team and to all the bloggers who work so hard to promote every author's work. Thank you, as well, to the usual suspects: friends and family, the team at Hot Tree Editing—especially Kristin S., CJC Photography, Najla Qamber, and the team at E.M. Tippett's Formatting.

Finally, thank you to *you*, the reader.

You met Chase Gartner in *The After of Us,* now read the prologue of his story, *I Stand Before You,* the award-winning first novel in S.R. Grey's bestselling Judge Me Not series.

I STAND BEFORE YOU

PROLOGUE

Chase

I LEAN my head back against the headrest, crank the passenger window down the rest of the way. The June night air rustles through my hair, reminding me I desperately need a trim. I run my fingers through the strands, chasing the path of the breeze.

My grandmother likes to lecture that I shouldn't have hair sticking out at odd angles, strands curling at the nape of my neck.

"You're such a handsome young man, Chase," Grandma Gartner said just this morning, *tsk*ing when I sat down for breakfast. "You look so much like your father did when he was your age. But, you know, *he* always kept *his* hair short and tidy." And then there was a pause, a long, dramatic sigh. She set down a plate of eggs — over easy — in front of me. "My poor Jack. God rest his soul." My grandmother crossed herself.

Her poor Jack, my father with the short and tidy hair — dead and gone.

I thought: *I am not my dad, Gram. He failed us, he gave up on us.* But the words never passed my lips. And they never will. Hearing them would only hurt my grandmother's feelings and she's too good to hear the angry thoughts poisoning my polluted mind. So I keep all that shit locked deep inside.

This morning was no different. I kept things light, said something like, "The girls like my hair like this, Gram. Got to keep the ladies happy, ya know."

Then I ducked and waited for the inevitable swat with the dish towel. But it never came. Instead, the lines in my grandmother's face deepened.

"You don't need to be concerning yourself with keeping ladies happy, young man. You're only twenty. Messing with women at your age will only lead to trouble."

I knew what she meant this morning, and I know it now too. She's worried I'll end up getting some girl pregnant. Then I'll be fucked, well and good. But I'm always careful, take the necessary precautions. Besides, it isn't my womanizing ways that's becoming a problem. If only. No, unfortunately, it's my ever-growing dependency on drugs—something my grandmother would never suspect—that has me worried these days.

These days… Yeah, right. More like these blurry, fucked-up segments of time.

Sighing, I roll the window up just enough to lean my head against the cool glass. *What am I going to do?* I silently ask myself.

What I really need to do is get the hell out of this tiny Ohio farm town I landed back in two years ago. I'm spinning my wheels here in Harmony Creek, hanging with a bad crowd. Problem is I have no plan, no money either. Drugs are my escape and have been for quite a while. My priorities are all fucked up. My life, it's upside down. Every day it seems like getting high—and staying that way—is my only goal. I want to stop—believe me I do—but I don't think I know how to anymore.

A lump forms in my throat at this thought, but I swallow it down. "Hey," I say to Tate, who is driving. "Let's get out of this town."

Tate Cody, my friend…and my partner in crime in

everything wild and crazy these days—women, drugs, drinking, fighting—you name it, we do it. And if we're not doing it nowadays, chances are we've done it at least once over the past couple of years. We've yet to slow down; we live on the edge.

I sometimes wonder when we'll fall.

"What do you think we're doing, Chase, my man?"

I take in and process Tate's reply, while he lifts a bottle of cheap gin to his lips and hits the gas. And for this one long, tortuous drawn-out second, I can't make a distinction between what I asked Tate and what I was only thinking. I panic, assuming my partner in crime's response is to let me know it's finally happening, we're really falling.

But then Tate adds, "I'm getting us out of here as fast as I can," and I breathe a little easier. He just means we're leaving Harmony Creek. Not falling, after all. *Shit, I need to ease up on the drugs.*

I glance out the window, and though it's dark I can see we're heading east, nearing the state line. Soon we'll be out of Ohio completely, and in the neighboring state of Pennsylvania. That's where we're supposed to hook up with two girls tonight. They're from New Castle, and we're meeting at a lake across the state line.

I don't really care about all that, though. What I'd really rather do is keep on going. Hop on Interstate 80 and clock the miles to Jersey. Better yet, Tate and I could go farther. We could drive our asses straight into New York-fucking-City. Now that would be sweet.

So while Tate barrels down a back road the police rarely patrol—until you get into Pennsylvania, that is—I pretend we're leaving Harmony Creek for good. No looking back, no regrets, just flying the fuck out of this lame-ass small town.

And speaking of flying, I'm flying a bit now too, feeling fine, baby, fine. I close my eyes so I can savor the s-l-o-w creep of numbness that cocoons me like a warm and fuzzy blanket.

I feel nothing, yet I feel everything.

My skin tingles a little, but when I touch my hand to my face it feels detached, like these parts of my body belong to two different people, neither of them me. That thought makes me happy, escape is exactly what I crave.

Needless to say, I've smoked—a lot—and not just weed. But it's the pills I swallowed a while ago that are starting to wrap me up and spin me the fuck out.

A bottle hits the back of my hand and my eyes fly open. Shit, I forgot I am not alone in this car.

"Drink, fucker," Tate urges.

I take the gin, despite the fact I can barely see straight. *No* isn't part of my vocabulary when I'm like this. And, sadly, more often than not, this is exactly how I am. This is who I am becoming: Chase Gartner, burgeoning drug addict.

As per most nights, Tate and I stopped at Kyle's before embarking on *this* night's little adventure. Kyle Tanner supplies us with more drugs than we could ever hope for. And the quality is always top notch. Kyle takes a certain kind of pride in dealing only primo product. But you'd never guess such a thing if you saw the rundown shithole he lives in.

Our dealer resides on the *other* side of town, over by the closed-down glass factory, in a clapboard house he shares with his meth-addicted dad. Lately, going there has been a contradiction of emotions for me. I love and hate concurrently when Tate and I cross over the railroad tracks that mark the end of the safe neighborhoods of Harmony Creek. Then, I vacillate between love and hate as I watch the Sparkle Mart grocery store appear…then disappear. I lean a little more towards hate when we reach the run-down apartment building where the junkies hang out, where their emaciated bodies lean lazily against the dirty brick exterior.

I sure as fuck don't want to end up there, God, no. But maybe I'm powerless to stop my downward spiral. Lord knows, by the time we start down the long dirt road that leads to Kyle's place, I crave and I want. And love trumps hate by that point. Even the junkies seem less scary. So we go…and we go…and we keep going back.

Tate tells me the road to Kyle's house is the road to salvation. *Salvation, my ass.* I'd be more inclined to say Tate and I are traveling a path to hell. We're in the express lane to damnation, and one step closer to burning every time we travel down that fucking dirt road. I know it, he knows it, but do we ever do anything to stop? Do we try to crawl out of the hole we're wallowing in? No, never.

In fact, Tate wants us to delve in deeper — start selling. He says we'll make, at the minimum, enough money to help pay for the copious amounts of shit we ingest…snort…smoke. Yeah, we do it all, everything short of needles. I somehow know if I ever cross *that* line, there will be no going back.

But I'm considering the selling thing, albeit for a different reason than my friend. Tate hopes to eventually make enough cash to buy his own wheels. He hates borrowing the piece of shit we're currently in — his mom's old, rusted Ford Focus. I just want to make enough money to buy a ticket out of this place. The little bit I earn painting people's houses, picking up construction work here and there — it's not adding up fast enough for my liking.

Hell, I still live at my grandmother's farmhouse out on Cold Springs Lane. Granted, I recently fixed up the little apartment above the detached garage, moved from a bedroom in the main house to an area not too much larger. But that little apartment provides privacy, and that's what I need. I am no longer a teenager, like when I first moved back two years ago. That's why I want, more than anything, to just get the fuck out of here. I'm thinking the money I make selling will make escape a reality, not just some pipe dream. No pun intended.

I raise the bottle of gin to my lips and tip it back. Alcohol heats my throat. "I think I'm going to take Kyle up on his offer," I say after I swallow the burn, the resulting grimace distorting my voice. "I need the money and it's going to take forever to earn it legit."

"You're making the right decision, my friend," Tate replies as he reaches over to take back the bottle.

Whoa... My vision turns wonky. There are three overlapping filmy images of my friend, and then just two.

"It's all about the numbers, man," two filmy Tates tell me.

I tell myself I need to slow down, and then I say to Tate, "That it is." I squeeze my eyes shut to keep from swaying in my seat. "That it is," I repeat.

The irony is that I once had money. Well, my family did, enough that my parents had a trust fund set up for me. Not a big one, mind you, but enough that it would've allowed for me to go to a decent college, get set up in a new city, shit like that.

I have no idea what my future holds nowadays, but I know it's been tainted by my past.

Back when I was around eight my parents moved from this town out to Las Vegas. My dad, who'd been successfully building houses here for a while, started a similar construction business out in Nevada. The timing was right, the stars aligned. We caught magic in the early days of the housing boom. Everything was golden and money poured in. It was happy times. For a while.

During those good times, Mom got pregnant. She gave me a little brother named Will that I still love like crazy and miss every fucking day. We used to talk on the phone all the time, but now I'm lucky if I get a two-word text from my little bro. I suppose when you're eleven years old — and haven't seen your big brother in two years — memories become a little hazy.

That's another thing the extra money from selling drugs will help with: I'll have enough funds to fly out to Vegas to see Will. Or I can just buy him a ticket to come here. As it is my mom, Abby, barely makes enough to get by out there.

But, like I said before, it wasn't always that way. In the early years, my father's construction company grew and thrived, so much so that I once entertained dreams of taking over the business. I used to imagine following in my father's footsteps, as sons are apt to do.

One afternoon, when I was about thirteen, I told my dad I wanted to build homes, same as he did. I showed him some sketches, just some basic designs and floor plans I'd thrown together. My dad was impressed. And not the false kind of fawning parents often try to sell to their kids. No, my drawings truly floored Jack Gartner. I could tell he couldn't believe his eldest son possessed that kind of crazy talent. He told me I should aim high, the sky was the limit. My sketches were incredible, he said, especially for my age. I could be an architect if I wanted, design skyscrapers even.

I had no reason not to believe him.

When you're thirteen you think you can have it all. Life hasn't roughed you up so very much…yet. At least it hadn't for me. So I told my father I'd do both — I would design the skyscrapers, and then I'd build them. My buildings would sell like hotcakes, and I'd be as rich as Donald Trump. No, richer even.

"The sky's the limit," I said, echoing my father's words back to him.

Dad smiled and patted me on the back.

Jack Gartner wasn't patronizing me, he truly believed in my possibility. "You have talent, Chase," he said. "Just don't ever lose yourself. If you can stay true to your dream...to who you are...then you'll do more than fly. Someday you'll soar."

Yeah, right. I sure am soaring at the moment, but I have a feeling this isn't what Dad had in mind.

Tate tries to pass the bottle back to me, but my mood has dampened. The pills, along with the memories, are doing a fucking number on my emotions. I'm sad one minute, reflective the next, mad at everything, contemplative over nothing. I guess I am officially fucked up.

I push the bottle away, harder than necessary, and clear liquid sloshes over the side. "Asshole," Tate mutters.

"Sorry," I say.

Do I really mean it? No, it's just a word, an empty string of letters. Empty, like me.

I tune Tate out. I am high as fuck and lost in my mind. We idle at a swinging red light hanging over an empty, dark stretch of road, and I sit waiting on an imaginary red light in my head, one on memory-fucking-lane.

When I blink, both lights turn green...

My dad started taking me to work the summer I showed him the drawings. I learned how to wire a home, how to put in plumbing, how to lay insulation. And that was just the beginning. I used to watch how my dad talked to the guys. He treated them with respect, and in turn they went the extra mile for him. It was all "Yes sir, Mr. Gartner," "Consider it done, Jack."

When I turned fourteen, my dad bought me a drafting table, a bunch of fancy software too. The kind real architects use, or so he said. I practiced all the time, got pretty damn good. I was building my wings, you see, preparing to fly.

Will was only five, but damn if that kid didn't love to sit around and watch me sketch. For him, I'd draw all kinds of ridiculous structures.

"Dwaw me a house, Chasey," he asked this one day.

I laughed while I tousled his blond hair. I remember the fine strands looked so light in the sunlit room. Hell, they were almost white. "All right, buddy, what kind do you want?"

"A house like a tweeeee," Will sing-song replied, green eyes innocent and wide as he focused on the sketch pad I'd picked up from my desk.

I readied a colored pencil and asked for clarification, "Okay, a tree house, right?"

"No-o-o." Will shook his little head vociferously. "A house that *is* a twee, Chasey."

"Aha, got it," I said.

And I did. I drew Will a tree house shaped exactly like a tree, big, sturdy, loaded down with bushy branches. The leaves I shaded in the color of my brother's eyes. I sketched a door at the base of the trunk, then drew a Will-sized truck and parked it under a low-lying branch. After I finished with some final shading, I held the drawing up for my brother to see.

Will's house looked like one of those tree houses in the commercials with the elves and the cookies, only this one I'd drawn was far better. There was a lot more detail, and I'd drawn the tree in 2-D. In among the branches and the leaves all the rooms were in cross-section, done up in varying shades of blue, Will's favorite color. I also made certain every last blue-shaded 2D-room overflowed with toys.

Will threw his arms around my neck and told me he loved his *twee house*. Then, he leaned back and told me he loved *me* even more.

He gave me a kiss on my cheek. That shit always touched my heart, choked me up a little. "I love you too, buddy," was about all I could say as I held on to a little boy who meant the world to me.

Things are never bad when love is abundant. I thought it would stay that way forever, I did. A home filled with love, a happy family, just a good and easy life.

Man, was I ever wrong.

Shortly after I turned seventeen my world began to crumble. The bottom fell out of the housing market. The wave everyone was riding touched the surf and crashed. My dad's business was one of the first to fail. He had overextended himself; all our assets were mortgaged. He made ridiculous deals, attempting to keep us afloat, but his efforts proved futile. We sunk faster than a stone.

I sold the fancy architect software on eBay, the drafting table too. I gave the money to my parents, but it was merely a drop in the bucket compared to what we owed. I watched my once-vibrant dad turn into a shadow of the man he once was. My mom, always so young-looking and pretty, developed dark circles under her eyes—from crying, worrying, not being able to sleep. She even tried her hand at the casinos, we were that fucking desperate. But everyone knows gambling is a loser's game. The house always wins in the end.

One night, my mom was at one of those casinos. It wasn't the first time she'd spent hours and hours away, trying to win back what we'd lost. She came out ahead a little here and there, but it was never enough, never enough.

Will had fallen asleep early that night, so my dad and I were more or less alone. He asked me if I was hungry. When I nodded slowly, reluctant to reveal just how ravenous I really was and cause my father any additional undue guilt, he sighed, picked up the phone, and ordered a bunch of Chinese take-out.

I swear I smelled that food before the delivery man even pulled up to the house. Beef Chow Mein, General

Tso's chicken, Hot and Sour soup, and eggrolls, the first real meal I'd eaten in weeks. And even though my dad and I had to sit on the floor—our furniture had been repossessed days earlier—I savored every fucking bite.

Afterward, my dad said he had somewhere to go. There was something he had to do. Would I keep an eye on Will?

"Sure," I told him while shoving white take-out cartons with little metal handles— leftovers I'd saved for Will and Mom—into the fridge.

With my father gone, I had nothing to do. Our TVs were gone, the stereos too. Video games? Forget it. Those were among the first things to go. So, I wandered around the house barefoot, padding around on neglected hardwood floors. I trudged from one empty room to the next.

Then I took a minute to look in on Will.

My little brother slept on an air mattress in the middle of his now-barren room. The *twee house* sketch, the only thing left on his four stark walls, had fallen. It lay abandoned on the floor, close to Will's hand, close to where his little arm was dangling off the side of the mattress. To me, it looked as if my brother was subconsciously reaching for the drawing. Three years had passed since I'd drawn Will's tree house—and I'd sketched hundreds of other things for him since that sunny day—but that particular piece of made-with-love art was still my brother's favorite. I think to him it symbolized something more. He'd once said my sketch gave him hope. I guess it reminded him of when things were good.

I stepped into his dark room and picked up Will's hope. I kissed the top of his head and gently placed his *twee house* next to his sleeping form. I made my way back down to the living room, feeling solemn and too fucking worn for seventeen. Tears welled in my eyes, but I refused to let them fall. *Hell with that shit.* The paper bag that had held the Chinese food was still on the floor. Frustrated, I kicked it out of my way. A fortune cookie shot out and landed at my feet. I picked the projectile up, ripped the plastic covering off, and slid a tiny piece of paper from the confines of the cookie.

The fortune stayed in my hand, the cookie ended up in my mouth.

Truthfully, I was still hungry. Crunching away and savoring sugary goodness, I read the words on the little slip of paper I held between my fingers.

As I stand before you, judge me not.

It sounded a little hokey and I almost threw the fortune away. But there was something about those words that made me hesitate, something almost prescient. I ended up folding the little piece of paper in half and tucking it in to my pocket. Maybe I needed some symbol of hope just like my brother. I knew the things happening in my life would eventually define my future, and I guess I hoped no matter what occurred those things wouldn't ultimately define me.

My mom came back later that night, but my dad never did.

Jack Gartner had gotten on route 160, heading west to California. But he never made it out of Nevada. His car was found at the bottom of a ravine, below what the officers who came to our door to break the news termed *a treacherous curve.*

Killed on impact, we were told.

Did he lose control, or drive off the road on purpose? Maybe his plan all along had been to leave us and start a new life in California. That's what my mom believed at the time. Still does, in fact.

I, however, am not so sure. My father didn't pack a thing. Sixty dollars and a cancelled credit card, that's all he had on him. I think my dad just gave up. He quit on us, and that was the way he chose to end it. My mom can delude herself all she wants, but I know in my heart that I'm the one who's got it right.

Anyway, the bank took the house soon after my father's death. My mom sold off what little was left. For a while, we became nomads in the desert. We lived in the only big-ticket item that hadn't been repossessed, a white minivan. The Honda Odyssey was home…until Mom won enough money gambling to move us into a cheap apartment. Our new residence was a dump, but at least it had running water. And it was furnished. Kind of.

When we first stepped across the threshold and Mom caught me scowling at the rusty fixtures, the water-stained ceiling, the musty olive-green carpeting, she tried hard to convince me our new place had its good points.

"Like what?" I asked.

"It's close to The Strip. That'll be convenient."

"Convenient for who?" I sniped. "You?"

"Chase," she said pointedly, "it's better than living in a minivan."

She had a point there, so we moved in the next day. Will's first reaction was to run straight to one of the two back bedrooms and hang up his tattered *twee house* sketch. I followed him and watched as he stood on a soiled mattress on the floor — in a shoebox of a room we were going to have to share — and pinned hope on a wall.

After we were settled, time, as it does, marched on. Will and I attended school, while my mom — still fevered and sick with the gambling virus — spent her days in the casinos.

I turned eighteen that April. But no one really noticed. Well, Will did. Not much got by that kid.

He stuck a candle he found in the back of a drawer in the kitchen on a stale snack cake. He made me sit on the only kitchen chair that didn't rock when you shifted, and then he placed the snack cake on a card table we used as a kitchen table.

Will sang me the most beautiful off-key and from-the-heart rendition of "Happy Birthday" that I have ever heard, before or since. When he was done, I leaned forward to blow out the candle. Will stopped me and told me to make a wish first, so I did. And then I blew out the candle. Will clapped and cheered. He asked me what I wished for and I told him it was a secret. I didn't want to tell him I wished for him to be given a better life than what we were, at the time, living. My brother and I split the snack cake in two, dinner for the night, and ate in contemplative silence.

Summer arrived that year and I somehow managed to graduate. But—with my trust fund long gone—college was no longer on the table. With no real guidance, and a lot of pent-up frustration, my downward slide took hold. I was angry all the time, and ended up getting into too many fights to count. The places in Vegas where I'd started hanging were tough. Early on, I got my ass kicked…often.

But then something happened.

I learned how to use my strength, my quickness, *and* my anger. I started to win. I had a real knack for fighting and rapidly turned into a badass nobody messed with. I earned street cred. All that really meant was guys started showing me respect and girls suddenly wanted to have sex with me. I happily obliged more than a few of the latter.

But all that shit meant nothing, I was empty inside. I had no one to talk to about the mixed-up emotions I didn't know how to deal with. Like, why was I so angry all the time? Why did I like to fight so much? Why did it feel so good to make someone else hurt?

But mostly I wondered why I missed my dad so much.

I missed talking to my father, seeing his face every day. I had relied on him, I still needed him. But he was gone. He took his own life. Why couldn't I just accept what had happened and forget him?

But I couldn't, and, worse yet, I longed for answers.

Every day, for a while, in my quest for enlightenment, I'd grab the bus outside our apartment and visit my father. Well, I'd visit his grave. At the head of where my father rested eternally, I'd sit under a big stone angel kneeling by his grave—thankful for the little bit of shade she offered under the hot, beating sun of the desert.

Sweaty and lost, I'd ask her if she could tell me why my dad wasn't still alive. Why had God allowed Dad to take himself away? Why did my father choose to leave me? Why would he leave Mom and Will too? Was our love not enough for him? Did he regret his decision when he realized there was no going back?

Of course, the stone angel had no answers, and one day I just quit going. No more sitting in the shadow of the angel, no more hot and beating sun. No more asking questions that could never be answered.

My trips to the cemetery were over, but that didn't mean I wanted to forget that *someone*—even though he'd left—had once believed in me. Despite everything, I still loved my father and part of me yearned to be just like him.

So, July of that year, I had his angel's likeness—the stone one at his grave—inked in profile on the middle of my upper back, between my shoulder blades.

I shift in the passenger seat now.

I can almost feel her back there, watching over me, like my dad's angel watches over him. And like his angel, mine is kneeling. The edges of her heavy robe lie in a puddle of fabric around her. Her wings are folded against her back. Her hair is long, obscuring the side of her face. And her head is bowed. In supplication or in shame, I haven't decided which. But if she's been watching the shit I've been doing these past two years, it's probably in shame.

After the angel tat healed, Mom hit for more money.

I successfully talked her into paying for another tattoo, guilted her into it really. In any case, I ended up with big, intricately detailed wings inked up and over my shoulder blades. The top feathers curve onto my shoulders, while the wings dip down the sides of my back, effectively framing the angel.

But the angel and the wings weren't enough. I wanted something more to remember my father, something to remind me always of that final night, when it was just him and me, eating Chinese food on the floor of an empty home, a last supper shared.

I kept coming back to the cookie, the fortune inside, the hope it symbolized.

As I stand before you, judge me not.

Words printed on a piece of paper, but really they were so much more. So I had those words inked—in concise and script letters—around my left bicep.

My tats were but temporal attempts to heal my soul, as my heart remained an open wound. There was no solace to be had at home. In fact, things were getting worse. I started to drink and do drugs to ease the pain and fill the void. I hated what had happened to our family. Seeing Will transformed from an energetic little boy to a sullen nine-year-old left me sad and frustrated. And watching my mother try to heal her fractured heart with gambling—and eventually men—just pissed me the fuck off.

But at least Mom wasn't indulging in one-night stands like I'd been doing. Nope, Abby actually went out on dates. Still, her attempt at dating led to a revolving door of boyfriends. Some lasted a week or two, some a little longer, but the one common denominator they all shared was that not a single one liked me.

Mom told me to try harder, give these guys a chance for her sake. I laughed and told Abby her men could blow me. "Chase, don't be crude," was her response.

By the end of the summer Mom hooked up with what turned out to be steady boyfriend number three. I was no fool; I immediately sensed my days were numbered. I would've had to have been blind not to see the writing on the wall, a wall I didn't realize I was hurtling toward. But it wasn't just Abby's lame new boyfriend disliking me that was a problem. There was something else, something she'd never admit to. There was no escaping it though, not really.

I saw Abby's problem every day when I looked in the mirror.

Standing in a cramped and steam-filled bathroom, hot water running, can of shave cream poised in hand, I couldn't deny the truth in front of me. I'd swipe at the misted mirror with my free hand, leaving it streaky, but mostly clear. And it wasn't me I saw in the reflection, it was my father. That's how much I looked like Jack Gartner, even at eighteen. And *that* was my mother's real problem.

Shit. Even thinking about it now — two years later — fucks with my head.

I glance over at Tate. He's quiet, taking long pulls from the bottle. I shift in my seat and wind up the window the rest of the way. Time to assess my bleary reflection, time to compare it to what it was, time to compare it to the man who made me…I sometimes do this just to fuck with myself.

When I take in my reflection, I laugh. Hell, the resemblance is still uncanny. And just like when I used to stare at the steamed-up mirror in the bathroom, it's my dad's eyes staring back at me now. But these pale blues are all mine. Yeah, *his* whites were never shot with red like mine.

Still, even with the bloodshot eyes, similarities far outweigh differences. Though it's not *short and tidy* — like Grandma Gartner would like it to be — my hair is the exact same shade as her son's once was, light brown. Jack also blessed me with his straight nose, his square jaw, and his defined cheekbones. Everyone used to say my dad was good-looking, I guess I am too. Girls seem to think so, that's for sure. And my mother sure was smitten with my dad.

Abby used to lean across the front seat of the sporty car my dad bought for himself during the good times. Will and I would be in the back, rolling our eyes at each other. My mom would kiss my dad, making him swerve a little as he drove. She'd tell him he was gorgeous, and that she loved him. Dad would laugh and tell Abby he loved her even more. He'd say his love for her burned hotter than the Vegas sun above us. My mom loved that shit. Will and I, however, would groan in disgust and make gagging noises.

Shit, I feel like gagging now. Not because of the memory, but at how closely I still resemble my dead father. I turn away from my reflection. I can't bear to endure this self-inflicted torture any longer. No wonder I was fucking sent away. Too bad I couldn't disappear completely just as easily right now. Guess, in a way, that's why I live my life the way I do, filling it with drugs…sex…violence.

Back then my very presence in my mom's life must have been a constant reminder of all she had lost. When you're striving to move on, you don't need an anchor to the past. She could move forward with Will, he was just a kid. Besides, he looked like her, not like my father. But I was eighteen, an adult, and far too much my father's son for everyone's comfort. I guess it was just too difficult for Mom to look at me—see *him*—and be reminded of all she'd once had.

So the day steady boyfriend number three, a guy named Gary, told her she could move in with him, I kind of fucking knew the invitation wouldn't be extended to me.

Sure enough, on a blistering hot afternoon, my mom sent Will out to ride his bike and told me we had to talk. She sat me down on the ratty couch in our shitty apartment. I felt like a condemned man waiting to hear his fate, and all the while the noisy air conditioning unit in the window behind me kept blowing gusts of lukewarm air across the back of my neck.

Not that it mattered. I barely noticed. I was mostly numb. In preparation for this "talk," I'd done a couple of lines of coke in my room. Of course, I hadn't brought that shit out until after Will had left. One thing I stuck to was that I never let my little brother see me taking part in any of my newfound vices.

Anyway, that day in the living room, I couldn't sit still. Fidgeting, fidgeting, tapping my foot. Mom took no notice, she was almost as bad. Pacing back and forth in front of me, smoking a cigarette, a new habit she'd just acquired. Gary smoked, so she'd picked up the habit too. *Pathetic*, I remember thinking.

My mother appeared so edgy and wired I almost asked her if she was dabbling in drugs, like me, or if what she had to say was really just that fucking bad. She started speaking before I ever got the chance.

"You're not a kid anymore, Chase," she began, still pacing, ashes peppering the olive-green carpeting.

She took a drag, crinkled her brow, and leaned over to stub her cigarette out in a plastic ashtray on a low table.

"You have to get started on doing something, somewhere, kid," she said as she spun to face me.

She stood right in front of me, and though my head was down I watched her every move. She blew out a breath and I watched her dark blonde bangs lift up off her forehead. A few strands stuck to her skin. Mom was starting to sweat.

"So, Grandma Gartner called the other day," she continued, her words deliberate, pointed, like a knife. "She said she's got lots of room in that old farmhouse back in Ohio. And she sure could use some company."

I looked up at her in disbelief. This woman who'd given me life tried to smile, but she could not. She knew damn well she was spewing pure bullshit. She just wanted rid of me.

"Just spit it out," I ground through clenched teeth, my voice far from even.

"Okay, of course, honey." She looked everywhere but at me. "Uh, so, Gram thinks moving back to Harmony Creek might do you some good, get you out of Vegas, give you a chance to start over, and—"

"Mom, I'm only eighteen. Start over?" I blew out a quick breath. "I haven't even had a chance to get started *here*."

Her expression grew stern. "Chase, don't act like I don't know the things you do behind my back." I tried to protest, but she shushed me. "I know you use drugs. I know you bring girls back when Will's not around. That shit isn't going to fly once we move in with Gary. He won't stand for it, Chase. He has standards—"

I snorted, "The fuck he does—"

"I'm not going to argue with you about it," she said, her voice tired and cracking.

When she reached for her pack of cigarettes, I noticed her hands were shaking. "Honey, I just think Grandma Gartner's is the best place for you right now, okay?"

I picked at a hole in my jeans. "Do I have a choice?" I asked, defeated, and, truthfully, feeling like I'd just been set adrift.

She shook her head no.

I'd known it was coming, but her words still flayed me up the middle and pierced my already damaged heart. I was shocked that my heart could continue beating, since it felt all smashed to hell. But beat it did. In fact, my heart pumped faster and faster, like it was going to burst right out of my fucking chest. Whether my reaction was from cocaine…or despair…I couldn't quite figure.

With my heart pounding like a sped-up death knell, I tried to push some words out of my cotton-dry mouth. "Mom…" I croaked, my voice catching.

I just couldn't finish.

Verbal communication failed me, so I tried to meet her eyes, speak to her soul. Was this really what she wanted? Send her eldest son away? Give up on me? Just like Dad did with all of us.

I searched and searched, but my mother had no answers in her big green eyes, no more than the stone angel had at my father's grave.

Abby took in a stuttered breath and turned away. She swiped at a tear. "It's for the best, Chase," she mumbled.

And then she left me sitting there, all alone, warm air blowing across the back of my neck.

I went back to my room and cut up three more lines.

That was nearly two years ago and here I am. Mom is still in Las Vegas with Will, on steady boyfriend number six, last I heard. She's still chasing the elusive jackpot too, hoping to recapture the life she once knew.

Good luck with that, I think bitterly. *Jackpot, my ass.* If anyone needs to hit a fucking jackpot, it's me.

Suddenly, drug-induced visions of flashing pots of gold swim lazily into my head, along with some break-dancing leprechauns, and I can't help but chuckle.

Tate looks over. He must think my mood has improved, 'cause he starts talking all excitedly about how much money we're going to make from our new business venture with Kyle. I listen to his voice, not really hearing any words, but then the cell buzzes and I am alert, very alert.

Tate tosses it my way. "That there would be the ladies," he says — all smooth like — as I catch the cell with one hand. Even impaired, my coordination is impeccable.

"Ladies, my ass." I roll my eyes.

Tate laughs, knowing as well as I do that the two girls we're meeting up with tonight are no ladies. They're looking for the same thing we are, but therein lies the beauty.

"What's it say?" he asks, nodding to the cell.

The text is kind of blurry, but, then again, everything is. I blink a few times and my vision clears. When I read it out loud, I mimic a high-pitched girl's voice, just to be an ass. "Crystal and I are almost at the lake. Come prepared. Tammy. Laugh out loud, winking smiley face."

"Dude-e-e." Tate shoots me a knowing sidelong glance. "You know what *come prepared* means, right? You got that covered, yeah?"

As reckless as I am — and that's pretty fucking reckless — I always make sure I wrap my shit up. Better safe than sorry. But as I feel around in the pockets of my jeans I realize I've left the condoms at home. "Fuck," I mutter.

The blue *Welcome to Pennsylvania* sign looms ahead, our headlights flashing off the reflective letters.

Tate asks, "What?"

I rake my fingers through my hair. "I forgot the goddamn things at home."

"Not a problem. We'll just stop at the convenience store across the state line."

"Bad idea," I counter. "Cops are always hanging out in there. You think they won't notice how fucked up we are?"

"How fucked up *you* are," Tate corrects, laughing. "I didn't smoke nearly as much as you."

"You smoked plenty," I mumble under my breath.

But Tate is right, I smoked more. And Tate smoked only weed. Plus, my friend didn't see the pills Kyle slipped me before we left.

Still, I nod to the almost-empty bottle. "You pretty much drank that whole thing, dickhead. You'll never pass a field sobriety test."

"Yeah, but I don't plan on taking one, my friend. And, I hide it better than you." He shrugs. "Trust me, I got it covered. Just wait in the car. It'll only take a sec."

Tate's always confident like this. He can talk anyone into just about anything. I always tell him he's a natural-born salesman. Maybe if we ever get our shit together he can do something legit using his smooth ways. It's cool, it's Tate's thing, and it helps make him popular. He's an okay-looking guy — brown hair, brown eyes, kind of skinny — but it's his smooth talk that gets him in with the girls. They eat that shit up.

We cross the state line, turn into the convenience store. No cop cars. "See, we're good," Tate says, still as confident as ever.

I flip up my black hoodie hood and slouch down in my seat. "Just be quick," I mumble.

Tate hesitates, and I know something is up. "What the fuck are you waiting for?" I ask.

He begins his sentence with "Don't be pissed —" and I cut him off right away, hoping I won't have to kick my good friend's skinny ass. It would be a damn shame really, since Tate wouldn't stand a chance against the likes of me. I am way bigger and far stronger, and the rage within me has no match.

"What?" I spit out, clenching my jaw.

Tate ignores my attitude; he's used to it. "I kind of need you to hold on to something while I go in there. Just in case."

"Just in case of what?"

I am running out of patience. I scrub my hand down my face, wary to hear what Tate the salesman is up to now.

He smirks, and I tell him to knock that shit off, save it for the "ladies."

"Okay, okay." He raises his hands in mock surrender. "I may have kind of asked Kyle to give us a little something to get our entrepreneurial gig started."

"Us?" I say, feeling the anger rise up. "You didn't even know I was going to sell with you until about ten minutes ago."

"What can I say, man." Tate places his hand over his heart. "I had faith."

"Whatever."

I try to stay pissed, because what he did was really out of line, but my anger fades fast. High as I am, these strong emotions are too fucking slippery to hold on to for very long.

Tate hands me a plastic packet filled with little pills, a rainbow of color. "Jesus." I know all too well exactly what this shit is. "X? You're fucking higher than I thought. We're supposed to start small, bitch. Move a little bud, see how it goes."

Tate shrugs. "We'll make more money this way. Like, I know we can sell to the girls tonight. Hell, I bet we can talk them into buying *our* hits."

He's laughing at his own ingenuity, but I ignore him. I'm too busy trying to count the pills in the packet. But being in the condition I am in, it's a bit of a challenge.

"How much is this anyway?" I ask, giving up on figuring it out for myself.

"Twenty hits," he tells me, and then he has the balls to throw another packet in my lap. "Make that forty…maybe a little more."

"You're fucking crazy. If we get caught, Tate, this isn't

possession. This is possession with intent to sell."

"That's why I'm leaving the shit here with you."

"Oh, that's real fucking cool." Back to being pissed, even my high can't calm me now. I whip one of the packets back at Tate. "I am so not getting caught with forty hits of Ecstasy, asshole."

"Calm down, man." He gingerly picks up the packet I've just thrown and holds it out for me to take back. "If a cop shows up just hit the road."

"What about you?" I ask as I grudgingly accept the X.

Tate grins. "Don't worry about me. You know I can play it cool. Just swing by after the heat's gone, and we'll be back in business."

"The heat? What is this, the seventies?" I ask, laughing, but Tate's already out the door.

I tuck the two packets of Ecstasy into the back pocket of my jeans and think nothing more of it. Until a few short minutes later when a state cop pulls into the lot. Then, I panic.

I start climbing over the console to get the fuck out of there, but, suddenly, with every fiber of my being, I know I've just made the dumbest mistake of my life. That, however, doesn't stop me from slipping down into the driver's seat, throwing the car into reverse. I hit the gas, peel out of the parking lot, and leave a cloud of gravel and dust in my wake.

I've got the Focus up to eighty, music playing…loud, loud, fucking blaring. Maybe I can outrun this cocksucker? I'm tapping my hands on the steering wheel along with the beat, flying so fast it's amazing I don't lose control and crash.

But I don't, I stay steady.

I even make it a good five miles down the road before a cop heading my way—backup, I'm sure—screeches to a wide arced stop in front of me. His patrol car blocks the entire road, so I have no choice but to hit the brakes and squeal to a halt.

My car ends up parallel to the cop car, both of us straddling the lanes, engines idling like we're in some fucking action movie. The air reeks of burning rubber, and smoke billows around us. The speakers beat out a song from 50 Cent that is frankly ironic at this point.

When all the smoke clears, the sign for the lake is right smack dab in front of me. I can't help but laugh. The shit situation I'm in, and all I can think of is that Crystal and Tammy are out there, waiting, for two boys who are never going to show.

Two more cops—including the one from the store— pull up behind me. I pitch the door open, tumble from the seat. I hit the warm pavement and try to stand. Someone yells, "Hold it right there, hands on your head."

I hear guns being drawn, cocked. This isn't a movie, I know they're loaded. I squint to try to see what's happening, but all the flashing lights leave me blinded. Before I can think another drug-muddled thought, someone tackles me from behind. My face smacks right into the yellow center line, but I don't feel a fucking thing.

Whoever tackles me yanks down my hood, frisks me, and comes up with my wallet. Oh, and the forty hits of X, of course.

It's all ambient noise from that point on, but I do hear, "Chase Gartner, you're under arrest."

I have no idea that, despite the altered state I'm in, these will be the last coherent words I will remember for a very long time.

The time following has no sense of structure. Days, weeks, they all blend together. I'm in jail, facing a long, long list of charges. But it's the X that has me fucked.

Bond is set high. I call my mom, but all she does is cry. Like, these horrible wailing sobs that do nothing but make my head ache more than ever. She keeps apologizing for not having the money and swears she'll help me when she can. I hang up. I won't be holding my breath. The past has taught me not to put too much stock into Abby's flimsy promises. Mirages in the desert are what they are—get too close and they disappear.

My grandmother wants to mortgage the farmhouse, all the property around it. We're talking a good fifty-five acres. It'd be enough to make bail, but I tell her *no way*. She's done enough for me already, and look at how I've repaid her. I don't deserve her money…or her love.

So I'm on my own. And not thinking very clearly. Once all the illegal shit is out of my system, I find myself in a constant state of agitation. I can't sleep, I barely eat. I sweat bullets even when it feels like I'm freezing.

Eventually all that passes, but then all I want to do is fight. Like beat heads in. It's worse than when I was back in Vegas; I feel so much more fucking rage. I sit around clenching my fists, hoping for a chance to kick some poor unsuspecting soul's ass.

Finally, my wish is granted.

They throw a cellmate in with me and my ass is on him like an animal, beating the hell out of this never-saw-me-coming sap. But then two guards see what I'm doing, pull me off the bloodied and broken man, and promptly return the favor.

Another blur of pain.

This one, though, I welcome. The medical staff gives me plenty of drugs, legal ones this time. And still more before I am put before the judge.

Even in the sedated fog I float around in, I quickly learn the law…and some new math.

MDMA, Ecstasy—X, as I like to call it—is a schedule I narcotic, and carries as stiff a penalty as heroin if you're caught dealing, which they naturally assume I was. Casual users don't tote around forty-plus hits of Ecstasy, but dealers do.

I say nothing one way or the other to dispel their myth, I rat no one out. I just stay quiet and accept my fate.

My math lesson continues…

Ten pills are equal to one gram, and I've been caught with over forty pills. Forty pills equal four grams, which is more than enough to be charged with possession with intent to sell. But I already knew that part, right?

My lesson isn't over though. It's only just beginning.

I learn in Pennsylvania, the state in which I've been apprehended, four grams can easily earn you a prison sentence. This is especially true when you don't have enough money to hire a good attorney. Add to that, your public defender isn't getting paid enough to care. Not that you're doing much to help the overworked, underpaid man do his job. And, oh yeah, don't forget that one prior arrest for fighting last fall. It didn't seem like much at the time, but it sure haunts your ass now.

Are you keeping up?

Some final math…

Four grams buys you a six-year sentence at a state correctional institute when you have no resources, and, really, no heart to fight it.

Twenty years of age feels like ninety when your freedom is stripped away.

It takes one hundred and forty-three steps to walk down a long, noisy corridor to reach cell block seventy-two.

And when they turn the key, you hear one life—the only one you've ever known up until now—ending.

"It's all about the numbers, man," as Tate would say.

It sure is, my friend. It sure is.

Continue the story…

Available on Amazon: amzn.to/1Ay7ACI